SOLOMON'S SEAL

BOOK TWO OF

THE
OGMIOS
DIRECTIVE

STEVEN SAVILE
AND STEVE LOCKLEY

Proudly published by Snowbooks

Snowbooks Ltd | email: info@snowbooks.com
www.snowbooks.com.

British Library Cataloguing in Publication Data.
A catalogue record for this book is available from the
British Library. Paperback / softback

ISBN: 978-1-911390-14-5

Secret Service Mandate 7266, otherwise known as the Ogmios Directive, sanctioned the formation of an elite team under the command of Sir Charles Wyndham. Their orders are to do anything and everything necessary to preserve the sovereignty of the British Isles. What that actually means is difficult to pin down. They are deniable. They act outside the law, removed from the security of the State.

If something went wrong they were on their own.

If something went right no one ever said thank you.

It was enough that when things went to hell, they were there. Sir Charles, known affectionately to his people as the old man, calls them the Forge Team, but their nickname amongst themselves is the Lost Cause.

They serve at the pleasure of Her Majesty and report to a faceless bureaucrat in the upper echelons of government known only as Control, though no one with the power to would ever admit that.

These five men and women are often the last hope.

PROLOGUE

Libya: Several Years Ago

Kasim placed the battered and twisted ring down on the table.

The dealer took it and held it up to the light.

He was sure that it was gold, and it was certainly old. It was not the first time he had been able to find work on a dig in the edge of the desert and managed to pocket one of the finds. Sometimes he could sell them, sometimes he couldn't. He wasn't paid enough to worry about the legality of what he was doing. He wasn't a fool, though. He knew the dealer wouldn't give him anywhere near a fair price for the ring, but money was money, and it came with no questions asked.

The dealer turned the ring over and over in his fingers: weighing it, judging it. It was obvious that it had been in the ground for a long time, but what constituted a long time? More than five hundred years? More than one thousand? Two thousand? Considering how long it had been down there, it was in decent shape. Although it had been badly dented and buckled, it was still clearly a ring. And in Kasim's mind, a ring made of gold that looked that old meant it was rare, and rare meant dollars.

"What will you give me? Dollar price?" Kasim asked while the dealer pondered his offer. The dealer raised an eyebrow. In that question, he learned more about Kasim than the scruffy little labourer could possibly have guessed: the desperate usually asked for payment in local currency—cold, hard cash they could take to the bars and gambling dens and blow through fast. Instant gratification. Anyone asking for dollars had a plan that didn't involve sticking around long term. The dollar guys were setting money aside for something special.

The dealer made a face. It was all part of the act. He was negotiating. He pursed his lips and shook his head slightly. "Fifty," he said.

Kasim reached out to take it back. "Fifty? You insult me, and you insult my mother and the camel that gave birth to her," Kasim said. "Five hundred."

"Five hundred?"

"It is old. Very. Old means valuable, and you know it. And it has the Star of David. There are enough rich Jews who would pay you a king's ransom for an artefact like this. Five hundred."

The look on the dealer's face convinced Kasim he was right.

"Perhaps you would like to find yourself a rich Jew then?" He didn't blink.

Kasim felt his heartbeat quicken. He had to hold firm. Stick to the figure he had asked for until the man increased his opening gambit. He couldn't be the one to weaken first. "Five hundred," he repeated for the third time.

"Tell me, did you pluck that number out of your arse? It is a nice number, I am sure, but you need to consider many things. You need to consider just how big a risk I will have to take to try to get this little trinket out of the country. I can't exactly sell it here, now can I? So that expense needs to be covered. Be reasonable. I am a reasonable man. Fifty is a good price."

"Fifty is robbery. Five hundred is a good price."

"I couldn't possibly. Too much. You are not being reasonable, Kasim."

Kasim remained silent.

He knew that he could walk out of there and sell it for more than fifty dollars without having to go more than a hundred yards. They both did. He waited. He was in a good position. This wasn't the only dealer in town.

The man turned the ring over on his fingertip, and then fished a jeweller's eyepiece from his pocket to go through the charade of pretending to examine it again. Kasim knew that he wasn't going to see anything he hadn't already seen, but it would give him the opportunity to make an improved offer without losing face. How much he offered now would determine the final price.

"Two hundred. Not a cent more. There's no margin left. It's a good price. Very good. Two hundred dollars, US. That's my final offer."

It wouldn't be of course, that wasn't how it worked. The fact that he had increased his offer so steeply gave Kasim confidence that he could get at least three hundred for the piece, and that was fifty dollars more than he had dared hope.

"Four hundred," Kasim said quietly but firmly.

He expected the dealer to counter, he didn't.

He nodded. "Four hundred; deal. I'll need to get the cash." He placed the ancient artefact down onto the well-worn leather table top and swung his chair around to face the antiquated capstan-lock safe behind him. Kasim couldn't quite believe how easy it had been, which meant the ring had to be worth far more than he'd demanded. How much more? Ten times? Twenty?

"A thousand," he said.

"What?"

"I've changed my mind. I want a thousand dollars for it."

"We have agreed a price," the dealer objected, swinging back around in his chair. He was clearly growing impatient. Kasim didn't care. There was more money to be had here.

"We both know that it is worth at *least* that much."

"We know nothing of the sort, Kasim. And greed is ugly. Four hundred. Have some honour. We both know that you would have settled for two-fifty; don't try and pretend otherwise. Be happy."

The dealer turned his attention back to the safe, and swung the capstan lock. He took a slim handful of notes out of the safe then closed the door of the safe again. Kasim couldn't catch so much as a glimpse of what lay inside, but in his imagination there were piles of banknotes and incredibly valuable artefacts like the one he was being robbed of. The dealer was a rich man. What was a thousand dollars to a rich man?

Kasim's hands were sweaty. He rubbed them dry on his cotton trousers.

One thousand dollars was more money than he had ever had. It represented a chance to build a better life for his family. The ring was his salvation. Who would ever have thought that a little bit of metal stuck in the ground would have the power to change his life?

The dealer turned to face him and with one hand counted out eight fifty-dollar bills onto the desk between them.

"What is this?"

"Four hundred dollars. It is what we agreed on."

"I said one thousand."

"I don't care what you said *after* we had struck our bargain, Kasim. That is just noise. Take the money and leave."

Kasim's hand snaked out to grab the artefact, but the dealer covered it with his own. "I said take the money."

"I don't think so," Kasim said, thoughtfully. "I will take it to someone else. Someone who appreciates what it is and will pay me what I deserve."

"That's what I was afraid you would say."

The silencer muffled the two bullets he fired into the Arab worker's chest. It was only when the second bullet hit him that Kasim realised that the dealer had shot him.

It was the last thought he had.

ONE

Nonesuch Manor, Outside London: Present Day

The screens showed the same picture over and over again: a symbol that was familiar to everyone sitting around the table at Nonesuch.

Two triangles intertwined.

"The Star of David," Sir Charles Wyndham said. It wasn't as though he needed to. Everyone at the table knew exactly what it was. "A symbol of the Jewish faith for thousands of years. Mr Lethe?" Jude hit one of the keys on the powerful touchscreen computer set into the table in front of him, and the images mutated into a different version of the triangles. This time they were overlaid rather than interlaced. "The image has changed little since it was first devised."

Ronan Frost sat quietly watching the briefing. He was immaculately dressed in one of his customary grand bespoke suits, no tie. It looked like he'd come in to the manor house after a night in an exclusive club. In contrast, Jude Lethe was in a worn-out Earthworm Jim T-shirt, and his puffy red eyes made it abundantly clear he'd just woken up. Konstantin wore a plain white V-necked T-shirt, no logo, no identifying marks, and blue denim jeans. Orla wore a pair of cut-offs and a baggy woollen jumper, and Noah might as well have been in a bin liner for the way the shirt hung on him, all rumpled and crumpled and smelling like he'd been sleeping in it.

The image changed again and again without really changing at all.

Recessed spotlights were set into the ceiling of the Crucible—that was what they called the briefing room. They were dimmed low.

Around the room, marble statuettes stood on plinths, each offering an aspect of war personified. There was Babd, the Celtic crow, and her sisters, Macha and Morrigan, the ghosts of the battlefield; Bast, the Egyptian lioness standing proud and tall, fiercely defiant, while the Greek Ares and the Roman Mars both wore the guise of hunters; one-eyed Odin, with the ravens Hugin and Munin on either shoulder, encapsulated fury and wisdom, wrath and beauty, the dichotomy of war itself; and, in the centre of them all, Kali, the Hindu goddess of death. The statuettes lent the room a curious air of the occult that the old man liked to foster. Although it wasn't the team's prime directive, a lot of what they did focussed around these kinds of artefacts.

"You dragged us in at five a.m. for a history lesson?" Konstantin asked. It was a reasonable question. Konstantin Khavin was a reasonable man. All he wanted was a reasonable answer. He knew Sir Charles' love of theatre and manipulation, but at five in the morning, he was just too damn tired to appreciate it.

"I wanted you to enjoy the dawn chorus," Sir Charles said wryly. "Now, the Star of David appears not only in Jewish history, but also in Christian and Islamic mythologies."

"Well it would, wouldn't it? They're Abrahamic faiths, they've all got the same root," Konstantin again.

Orla Nyrén couldn't remember the last time the taciturn Russian had spoken even half as much. He listened and he acted; he didn't debate. He didn't make jokes. That was Noah.

"Indeed they do, though it was not King David, but rather his son who was most closely associated with that symbol."

The team waited for the punch line. They weren't the kind of people to play teacher's pet. No one was going to answer the unspoken question. The old man let out a snort. Like a picture, a snort was worth more than a thousand words.

"King Solomon," he said at last. "I trust you've all heard of him. How about the Seal of Solomon? Mr Lethe, if you would do the honours." Jude advanced the slide show again, this time bringing up an artist's impression of a gold ring bearing the emblem. "According to the legends, Solomon's ring bore the name of God on the gold band, and was used to capture and bind at least one demon."

Noah sniggered, but there was no hint of a smile on the old man's face. "You may well laugh, Mr Larkin, but I would have thought that you of all people would be open to the idea that it's not the notion that something has magical properties, but rather that people *believe* that it does, that is important."

"Exactly: primitive, superstitious minds. But no one is going to believe in magic over science or reason now. We're out of the Dark Ages. We've been enlightened." Sometimes it was easy to forget that Konstantin was from Eastern Europe. It had been many years since he had set foot on communist soil, but every now and then his heritage came to the fore. He was raised in a world where religion was suppressed, and he was just contrary enough to be fascinated by alternate belief systems. And of course, there were enough religious fanatics in the world that would kill for this cross or that sickle or the other star, that knowing what motivated them was useful.

"You say that," the old man said, "But in the UK census of 2001, almost four hundred thousand of our enlightened citizens registered their religion as Jedi."

"But that was a joke, wasn't it?" Orla said, looking at Jude Lethe as though she suspected he was somehow behind the whole thing. It was the kind of joke he'd think was infinitely funny, but he was hardly likely to hack into the census computers and fiddle the numbers just for fun.

"Of course it was," Lethe said, shaking his head.

"Joke or not, it was more than three times the number the Church of Scientology laid claim to a few years later." Sir Charles noted. "So enlightenment, superstition, humour, it's all relative. Mr Lethe, if you'd be so kind?"

Jude changed the image again, this time it was of a genie trapped in a bottle.

"In 'The 1001 Nights', Scheherazade recounts a tale of a djinn trapped in a bottle that is sealed with the symbol," said Lethe. "Which illustrates how myths and legends get used and reused over time."

"Fascinating, I'm sure," Noah said. "But can we fast forward about an hour to the bit where we come in?"

Sir Charles didn't miss a beat. "All in good time. It would appear that a ring has surfaced, and the right people believe that it could well be Solomon's Seal. And regardless of supposed magical powers, it would certainly be the oldest surviving example of the symbol, meaning a lot of people with a lot of money would want to get their hands on it. People from both sides of the divide."

Orla knew only too well what he was talking about when he said the divide: Arabs and Israelis, Jews and Muslims. Each would want it for their own, but more importantly, they would want it so that it couldn't fall into the hands of their enemies. Fanatics on both sides would rather see the thing destroyed than have it fall into the other's possession.

"Do we know where it is now?" Orla asked.

"Occupied Palestinian Territories, The West Bank, Gaza, if our latest information is still current. There is, of course, a strong chance that it will have been taken into Israel."

Orla didn't say anything. Israel was her area of expertise. It was where she felt most comfortable—and where she was most valuable.

"The internet is rife with rumours about it," Jude Lethe explained. "It seems that it may have been stolen from an archaeological dig by a local labourer. The find was catalogued as 'ring: unknown origin'. I've managed to locate the cataloguing photograph, showing it in the state it was found, which as you can see is basically unrecognisable, and then again after a cursory dusting." Lethe called up the next images.

The picture on the left was of what appeared to be a piece of sandstone with the tiniest sliver of metal protruding from one edge, while on the right the stone, sand and dust had been carefully eased away to reveal a piece of twisted metal.

At first glance it looked like gold, but Orla couldn't be certain. She looked at the image with her head inclined slightly, as if that would help her to get a better view of the symbol. She needn't have tried so hard. Lethe changed the image again, this time offering a close-up of the symbol.

"It disappeared before it could be sent away to the university labs for a more thorough analysis."

"So this is just guesswork," Noah observed.

"Not *just*. But, as much as the ring's supernatural powers are of no consequence, when belief comes into things, it is whether or not people believe that this is Solomon's Seal that matters. If they do, then to them, that's exactly what it is."

"And that makes it worth killing for," Konstantin said flatly.

"Exactly," Sir Charles agreed.

"And it isn't as though people need any more excuses for that," the Irish man, Ronan Frost, spoke up for the first time. Frost, it seemed, had taken on the strong silent archetype Konstantin had left behind.

"If the Jews and the Arabs believe this thing is genuine... it doesn't bear thinking about," Orla said. Too many wars had been fought with religion as an excuse: always an excuse, but rarely a reason.

"You said that this was from an archaeological dig?" Noah leant further back in his chair. Something had piqued his interest.

"That's correct," he said flipping through a few images that showed a fairly large-scale dig, and then a map offering its relative position. "It's a German operation."

"Libya? So the ring wasn't unearthed in Palestine?" Noah asked.

"Occupied Palestinian Territories," Jude corrected.

"You say tomato."

As far as Orla knew, none of the team was a Libyan specialist.

"The fall of Mu'ammar al-Qaḏḏāfî's regime has meant that archaeologists have begun to get access to places which haven't been examined for a long time. Treasures are being discovered—and of course, disappearing again—every week. While locals will work for peanuts, they appear to be embracing the notion of Finders Keepers quite readily."

"So the Germans got their towels on the ruins first," Noah said.

"Indeed they did."

"But why Libya?" Orla had her suspicions, but maybe the answer wasn't as obvious as she thought.

"The primary excavation is of an ancient Roman settlement, but the area was also occupied by the Moors. We don't have any firm idea of how the Seal might have got there, but there is plenty of evidence of material moving across North Africa through the periods of both civilizations."

"So how did it make the journey from Libya through into Palestine?" Orla asked. There was a certain kind of rightness about the idea of an artefact going home, a symmetry that seemed fitting. She couldn't see why the team were being asked to get involved in this: unless the old man knew stuff he wasn't revealing.

"Whispers. Rumours. Nothing concrete."

"Then we should get us something concrete." Konstantin said, ever practical. There was something methodical about the way his mind worked. Everything fitted into an order—a structure—that made logical sense. Nothing was left to chance. It was the Russian way. Konstantin rarely showed any signs of impatience, and yet here he was, gnawing at the bone.

Orla glanced at the big Russian.

She looked at the old man.

His face was unreadable, as ever.

But that only served to strengthen her suspicion that this was a 'devil makes work' operation to keep them occupied. Still, it would be good to get out in the field; things had been quiet for months. As far as she was concerned, there was one thing worse than facing death every day, and that was staring down boredom.

And boredom brought other problems, any one of which could be lethal out in the field if you let discipline slip.

"Okay," Ronan Frost said, finally leaning forward. He'd heard all he needed to hear—or had been briefed before the rest of them had arrived. It wouldn't have been the first time. Frosty was Sir Charles' right hand. "Let's go back to the beginning. Forget rumours. Rumours could easily be false trails laid down by someone not wanting us to find the Seal. We know where the ring was found. Do we know anything about the man who found it?"

Sir Charles nodded. "While we can't completely discount the archaeologists and the students working the dig, it is reasonable to assume they have more to gain by the find becoming public than they do from it disappearing into the hands of some private collector. Which leaves the local day workers. They come and go. Some are there for a few days at a time, and then disappear for two or three more before returning again. Our man on the ground has done some digging of his own, and it seems one man was with the crew almost from the beginning. This isn't unheard of, but what makes him interesting is he hasn't been seen for a couple of weeks. It's reasonable to assume his disappearance fits the timeframe of the ring's theft."

That was it: that was the one solid thing to hang everything else onto. People couldn't disappear half as well as the T.V. and movies made it seem. Especially not normal people. This local worker wouldn't be covering his tracks, and even if he were, he wouldn't be able to cover them well enough.

"Name, last known address? What have we got?" Frost asked.

"The man's name is Kasim Hamid." The screen changed again, bringing up a blurred picture of a young Arabic male. It looked like a messy photo fit.

"Is that the best you can do, Jude?" Frost asked.

"It's not always as easy as CSI makes it look, mate," the tech-wizard replied.

At least he hadn't made a joke about them all looking the same—not that it would actually have been intended to be racist. Lethe was just fixated on the tech, and one man in Arabic desert dress would look a lot like many other men in Arabic desert dress when viewed through the enhanced satellite imaging. It wasn't as though Kasim Hamid had passed in front of a CCTV camera. These images originated up in orbit; even getting a semi-usable likeness was a miracle of modern technology.

"So what do we know about this guy?"

"Age twenty-seven, married, with two children. No record of problems with the authorities, but given the regime change, that isn't necessarily the full story. Petty crime isn't high on anyone's agenda at the moment. But, from the little we've found, he seems like your average working stiff. His supervisor on the dig described him as hardworking and unremarkable. That's pretty much all we have on him so far. Unfortunately, when you're dealing with a country where the vast majority of the populace don't even hold a driving license, never mind a passport, the legitimate paper trail can be a little on the thin side. Luckily, I'm good at what I do: I've got an address for him and the name of a previous employer. Now it's down to you guys to hit the ground running."

Orla was already thinking about how difficult it would be for her to get into Libya and dig up everything there was to dig up about Kasim Hamid. It wasn't ego. She knew that Sir Charles would want to send in the best person for the job, and that was she. She was the Middle Eastern Expert on the team. Her education, language skills and proficiencies meant there was only one logical person to do the spadework.

"He could be a small cog in a much larger machine," Frost offered. "Or, more likely, he's lying in the desert being chewed over by the animals."

Sir Charles grimaced at Frost's grim assessment, but both scenarios were possible: criminal mastermind or dead dupe. If he'd been a gambling man, he would have put it all on dupe.

"Kasim's the only lead?"

"No. We have the other end of the chain," the old man said. "Or at least where I believe the chain might lead. This is all supposition. But it's backed up with solid Intel."

The image on the screen changed to a picture of a group of men in desert fatigues. The man in the middle was familiar; the others were less so. The man closest to him—with a patch over one eye and a scar along one cheek—looked like something out of a comic book villain catalogue.

The Beast.

"General Youssef Saddiq," Konstantin said. "One-time military leader in Northern Iraq."

"Trained by the Russians," Orla added.

"Nothing more than a power crazy has-been," said Noah.

"More like a religious nutcase," Lethe said.

"He most certainly is all of the above," said Sir Charles. "And then some. It's a dangerous combination. We've had solid information that he's ready to take receipt of the ring very soon, if he hasn't already got it."

"Intentions? Is he looking to start a war, or set himself up as a messiah? I mean, does he believe the ring's magical and can vanquish demons?"

"Saddiq is a dangerous man. He's also a clever man. There's nothing more worrying from our side of the fence than a clever, dangerous man. He doesn't need to believe the ring's magical—he just needs other people to believe in it."

"If it were me, I'd give people the evidence they need to believe it's magical: do something spectacular, and blame it on the ring," Lethe said.

"Right: give the people what they want, play to the peanut gallery," Noah agreed. "Something big and showy. But what the hell could you blame on a bloody demon?"

"The possibilities are endless," Orla said, and counted off a handful from the top of her head for them. One snagged in her mind: "A plague on the people of Israel. It isn't hard to release a pathogen and blame it on God. But that isn't the man's style." The man. She couldn't even bring herself to say his name. He was just the Beast. The beast she had promised herself she would kill.

"A dirty bomb," Sir Charles said.

That *was* his style.

TWO

Libya: Present Day

There was something about looking for a missing person in a strange country that made rooting around for a needle in a haystack an attractive proposition.

At least with the needle-in-a-haystack, the whole conceit was built around it actually being in the haystack somewhere. Sooner or later, you'd turn it up if you searched diligently enough, even if you had to unpick every single piece of hay and discard it.

This was different.

Frost wasn't an optimist. He knew he was looking for a man who wasn't there. Kasim Hamid was pushing up daisies, he was sure of it, and digging around was only going to trip red flags and eventually tip off either Kasim's cohorts, or his killers.

He could have written what he'd learned on the back of a postage stamp and mailed it home—without the aid of a microdot. The theft was supposedly being dealt with by the local law enforcement. Two minutes poking around convinced Frost they were worse than useless. Useless he could work with. Corrupt, he couldn't. As far as the officer leading the investigation was concerned, there was no difference between one of the locals liberating the ring and what the Germans had been planning to do with it. Libya was losing a piece of its heritage either way. At least this way, one of their own was making the money.

Kasim's family were still living in the small apartment he had given the dig as his home address. In an ideal world, Frost would have watched their comings and goings for a day or two, assuming that if Kasim were alive, they'd lead him to him eventually. But the world wasn't ideal. He was going to have to engineer a situation where he could ask Kasim's wife the questions he needed to. Her phone records didn't list any international calls, any hotels or curiously short calls/hang-ups. Added to that, the fact that it had been a week since the theft, and she hadn't taken the family out of the area, made Frost think she didn't know where Kasim was. And that made him suspect it wasn't a planned theft. It was a rare man whose wife couldn't read him like a well-thumbed book, no matter how clever or devious he thought he was. The women always knew.

Frost took a deep swallow from the café latte that was now lukewarm. He'd chosen the café because one of the languages it claimed to be able to take orders in was German. His accent wasn't good enough to fool a German, but it was good enough to pass for native in conversation with someone who had a smattering of German as his or her third language. And he knew enough about people to know that someone would walk through the door who either worked on the dig, wanted to work on the dig, knew someone who worked on the dig, or just wanted to show off to the foreigner. It was human nature. So he ordered loudly enough for his voice to carry, and deliberately didn't open a newspaper. He wanted to appear approachable. Newspapers put you into a world of your own.

It was all about invisible barriers. Even so, it took longer than he had expected for a man to approach his table.

It was already the middle of the afternoon.

"May I join you?" the man asked in fractured, slightly hesitant German.

Frost looked up and offered a smile, as though he were a veritable fisher of men. There were vacant tables in the café. He looked over towards the counter, where the waiter made himself look busy.

"Be my guest."

"Are you here for the excavation?" the man asked.

Frost nodded. He didn't offer any more information than that. It wasn't his story he was interested in. He wanted his new friend to do the conversational legwork. He couldn't exactly say, "Hey, I am here to sell stolen artefacts. Form an orderly queue to get your sacred relic." No: a slight air of suspicion was good, and it wouldn't deter a black-marketeer.

They made fairly easy, not-too-specific conversation about what was going on out in the desert for ten minutes or so, Frost carefully avoiding too much detail, so that he couldn't trap himself in a lie or give away that he hadn't actually been there.

Ten minutes became fifteen.

Fifteen became twenty.

The man seemed to be growing a little more agitated as time wore on. It was cute, like a nervous boy gearing up to ask the pretty girl out on a date, but expecting her to say no. *Here it comes*, thought Frost.

"It must be difficult," the man began. "Morally, I mean."

"How so?"

"Deciding what happens to our heritage."

"Oh, I don't make any decisions. I do what I do for the good of everyone."

"I'm sure you do. Absolutely. Obviously. But what I mean is, some things you unearth will inevitably be culturally significant."

"I would hope so. That's why I do it, after all."

"Yes, yes, but sometimes, well, if you happen to come across something of cultural *value,* something you think ought to remain here, for the good of my country and her people, well, I have friends who would like to make sure our treasures remain here. I could always arrange for you to receive a finder's fee for your trouble, of course," he said at last.

A finder's fee? Well that's certainly a politically correct way of putting it, Frost thought.

"Do you work for the Department of Antiquities?" Frost asked, knowing that there was no such governmental department out here. He assumed the man knew that, too, but it didn't stop him.

"A friend of mine does. I could introduce you to him."

"That's very kind of you." Frost said, carefully. He tried not to sound too eager. He wasn't here to ferret out governmental corruption. He didn't care who was greasing what wheels to forge the necessary documentation to smuggle antiquities out of Libya. He was only interested in Kasim Hamid and the ring. To that extent, his new black-marketeering friend was no more than a means to an end. If Kasim had gone through one of these 'brokers', the odds were good that they'd all funnel back to one source. Frost wanted to meet that man.

"It's my pleasure. I could take you to see him now if you like, just so that I can introduce you."

Frost looked at his watch. His shirt was dry now. In five minutes he'd be sweating like a pig and willing to trade his unborn for a cold drink. It had to be the hottest part of the day.

"His office is not far from here. We can walk there in five minutes." Frost nodded. Walking meant discomfort. He'd have done the same thing in their place. Put him at a disadvantage; make him sweaty and uncomfortable before sitting down to do business. It wasn't what they taught you at Harvard Business School, but it was effective. The introduction was too quick though, too easy, and that meant he'd have to be on his guard.

But then again, he always was.

That was what had kept him alive through the Troubles.

THREE

She had been back before, but not here. Not Palestine. And even though it didn't exist on any political map, it was still Palestine to her.

Israel was one thing, even with the horrors of the Beast and everything that had happened to her there, but it wasn't Palestine. It wasn't Jenin.

And she had genuinely hoped she would never set foot on Palestinian soil ever again. It was hard enough flying into Israel, but crossing over into Palestine? Palestine was the stuff of her nightmares.

Orla had flown into Ben Gurion Airport on a budget airline along with far too many orange-skinned, blonde women weighed down by an excess of tacky gold jewellery. This wasn't exactly Stag and Hen territory. She could have flown in on the private jet, but that would have brought a different kind of attention. This way, she could just slip into the country without raising any flags. She was just another bargain tourist.

She wasn't going into the lion's den alone.

Sir Charles had pulled a few strings with Control and arranged for Konstantin to hitch a ride on a military flight into Atarot Airport without popping up on the passenger manifest. Atarot had been closed to commercial flights since the second Intifada, when the runways had been half-buried in stones thrown by Palestinians. Military aircraft were made of sterner stuff. Despite the bumpy landing, he'd probably have the more comfortable flight.

Orla checked her watch.

His flight would be in the air, but still seven hours out, leaving her plenty of time to do everything she needed to do before they rendezvoused.

Sir Charles had cleared it for a one-man operation with Israeli support, into and out of Palestine with the aim of bringing down Saddiq. She didn't know how he'd done it. She didn't ask. Sir Charles was connected in ways that didn't bear thinking about. Of all the men she'd ever met, he was the only one who frightened her—and she loved him like a father.

Mossad had tried twice and failed twice to neutralise Saddiq. They'd sent a nursery after him—that was an entire hit squad who'd failed to finish him off, though they had caused a diplomatic incident when they blew up a diplomat's car in Tel Aviv, mistakenly thinking it contained their man. Saddiq had played them, and the Israelis didn't like that. It wasn't common knowledge. They didn't admit to failures.

An Eastern European going in alone was a different matter. If he succeeded, then they were rid of a problem. If he failed, he was deniable.

They had nothing to lose.

Orla was the old man's ace in the hole. Mossad didn't know she was going in, though once she passed through customs, it was only a matter of time. That was where Jude Lethe came in. She had no idea how he did what he did, but he'd assured her he'd got a contact in Israel who was able to suppress the red flag on her passport. He wasn't willing to risk taking it off in case that triggered some other safeguard, but with luck, he'd buy her a day. She'd find out whether he was full of shit soon enough.

Orla walked into the wall of heat and fumes as she stepped through the aircraft door. She'd done the hard part: she'd come back to Israel. It was going to be different this time, she assured herself.

She didn't believe herself for a second.

Even at this time in the morning, the heat was almost insufferable after the air conditioning of the pressurised cabin. Still, the fumes were blessed relief from the stink of cheap perfume and alcohol that coated the Essex girls like a smog of bad taste.

Orla fished her passport from her bag and tagged onto the back of the gaggle of drunken girls. Groups were always less noticeable than a single woman travelling alone. She needn't have worried; the immigration staff ushered them through as quickly as possible. The sooner they were through, the sooner they would be someone else's problem. It was written all over their faces. She would probably have felt the same in their position. Drunken women were a nuisance; they weren't a threat to national security.

One of the more sober girls turned and gave her a glance. She smiled as though she was trying to remember if Orla was part of their group—a friend of a friend, maybe?—and tried to draw her into the sacred circle. Orla smiled back and moved just a little closer, but not close enough to actually have to talk, until they were heading out of the terminal.

The big advantage of the budget airlines was that most of the passengers travelled light, using carry-on luggage rather than pay the extra cost for a proper suitcase in the hold. Orla always travelled light. It was easier to move on in a hurry if you weren't worrying about packing. A couple of the more drunken hens giggled lecherously when they saw a man holding up a cardboard sign that said he was there to take them to their destination. Orla peeled away from the group and headed over to a car rental desk.

Within twenty minutes she was behind the wheel.

She had six hours until Konstantin landed.

FOUR

The touchdown was brutal.

Military pilots came down *hard*. They wanted the wheels on the ground and weren't worried about their passengers. Military pilots landing on rough terrain didn't take chances. The stones that had been thrown by Palestinians in defiance of Israeli occupation all those years ago had been cleared away just as long ago, but the damage done to the landing strip had never been repaired. That kind of thing might give the civil aviation authorities pause, but these guys were made of sterner stuff.

Konstantin Khavin slung the rucksack over one shoulder and made his way down the landing stage. The steps had been driven into place even before the turbines of the engine had stopped turning over.

Konstantin kicked the ground as he stepped onto the tarmac. His boot sent a pebble skidding across the ground. He looked around. Some signs of conflict never went away. There was no welcoming committee. That was good; he didn't want to waste words explaining himself. He wanted to hit the ground running. Time was of the essence. Palestine lay on the far side of the perimeter.

There was a jeep waiting for him.

The driver had been briefed to take him to a safe hotel.

Mossad had made the arrangements.

He was to wait there until an operative from the Palestinian side of the border made contact. They'd offered to take him over, but he'd declined. There was too much distrust and suspicion on both sides. They'd only get in the way. The Israelis were concerned Konstantin would blow their man's cover if he openly tried to help him infiltrate the area. Konstantin was certain the Palestinians knew exactly who the Israeli spies were, even if they let them think that they remained unidentified. That was just the game. So he let them think he was playing along, but the last thing he intended to do was sit in some stuffy hotel room waiting to be picked up. And he wasn't about to go over any recognised border crossing. Too obvious. Too dangerous.

The jeep dropped him off at a high-end hotel in the heart of the city.

It would have been tempting to grab a few hours shut-eye but for the fact that he'd already made two sets of eyes on the place. If he walked through that door, *he* was made, and the Israelis would know his every move.

He thanked the driver, but didn't get out. "Drive," he said.

The man seemed confused.

Konstantin reached across and grabbed his kneecap, digging his fingers in under the bone and pushing down. The car lurched forward. He squeezed hard. "Drive." This time the man understood. He pulled out into traffic. Konstantin watched the panicked reaction of the two men he'd made as they tried to react to the change of plan. "Faster, or you'll never walk again." The driver floored the accelerator. They had been moving for less than six minutes when Konstantin barked, "Here." And the man slammed on the brakes.

Konstantin was out of the car in a second, rucksack slung over his shoulder. He disappeared into a warren of streets that would lead in turn to the poorer districts. He wanted an out-of-the-way hotel—preferably the kind of place that rented rooms out by the hour. The kind of place where the reception clerk forgot your face the moment you walked through the door.

Not the kind of place where tourist buses pulled up outside.

He booked a room for a week under the name of John White.

In the room, he tossed the rucksack on a bed with cigarette burns like pox scars and looked out through the grime-stained windows. Despite the history that lay in its stones, it wasn't one of his favourite cities. The view from the window showed the sidewall of another building just a matter of feet away. He could have reached out and touched it. He had stayed in a lot of rooms like this. It was worn and tired and not particularly clean.

He sat on the bed. The springs offered no resistance. They creaked and groaned under his weight. It was the kind of noise that would easily carry to the adjacent rooms, which didn't make him long for darkness, given the chorus of the sex that would accompany the moon.

He checked the digital clock on the bedside table. Orla was about to make the crossing into Palestine, less than a mile from where he was sitting. Everything hinged on her being able to travel through the country unseen.

He went back to the window and pressed his face against the glass. He would have got a better view of the alley below if he'd opened the window, but it had been nailed shut. Even with the restricted view, he was confident there was no one out there.

He couldn't have chosen a better room, though: the iron fire escape was just about within reach from the bedroom window—once he'd prised the nails out—so he could come

28

and go as he pleased without the risk of setting off emergency exit alarms in the corridor. And if worst came to the worst, he could evacuate the room in a hurry without having to go through the front desk.

Mossad were good; they didn't lose their men. Not here. It wasn't as though he could disappear. Not for long. They'd find him soon, but that was okay. He expected them to. And he expected them to break into his room and rifle through his belongings. It was just procedure. A dance. Rather than giving them the slip, it was just so much easier to manipulate what they found when they conducted their search. It wouldn't satisfy them, but short of mugging him on the street to check his pockets, it was the best they could do.

Of course, after his little stunt with the driver, he wouldn't have put that past them. Konstantin removed a couple of the items from the rucksack and slipped them into his pocket. He put a mobile phone down on the bedside table. This wasn't his regular phone. Lethe had arranged for a spare, filling it with innocuous numbers and a false trail of messages that bore as much resemblance to real life as the last *Mission Impossible* movie. It was all about watching the watchers: the phone was sound-sensitive. Any sound over a pre-set register would trigger the camera to record sound and vision. You never knew what people would say if they didn't think they were being watched.

The last thing he did before he left the room was send a text to Lethe, who would forward it to Orla's burner phone.

Done, he left the room.

Konstantin nodded to the guy on the reception desk, and almost as a second-thought asked him if there were any restrictions on the door key.

"Reception's manned twenty-four seven," the man said. "Outside door locks at eleven, so you'll need your room key to get you buzzed through."

"Thanks," Konstantin said. Mossad agents would question the man when they came calling. He'd remember the Russian asking about the time the main door closed, and that would make them think he was going to be gone well into the evening. That suited him just fine.

The primary advantage of coming into the country via military transport was that his belongings hadn't been searched—not before he left the UK, or when he arrived in Israel. He'd made the entire journey without once having to prove his identity, never mind produce his passport.

He found the café.

It was small and intimate. There were eight diners. Two sat in the corner, backs to the wall, with a good view of the door. Three sat alone. The remaining three, who on first glance he would have taken for students, sat together, animatedly discussing something no doubt of earth-shattering importance. They weren't students. There was no single giveaway, just a lot of little tells: the paper in the ring binder in front of the girl was unbroken, meaning the pages had never been turned, let alone written on; the ink in the three biros scattered across the table top was full—three different people, each working with the same brand of pen, and none of them having been used before was more than coincidence. It was sloppy. Insulting. They were agents. And they'd made his meeting even before he had.

He thought about turning around and walking out. It would have been the smart thing to do. Then he thought about taking the 'students' out back and giving them a beating, just to send a message back to their 'Father'. But that would only cause more trouble than it was worth.

There were as many empty tables as occupied ones. They were each laid with a fresh white linen tablecloth. He pointed to one near the window, where he could position himself with his back to the wall to prevent someone being able to move on him unseen. The waiter nodded. It would only take a brief "Hi" in English or a *"dobryj dyen'!"* in Russian, and someone who was able to speak either would come bustling out to take his order. That was the whole wonder of global commerce. Once the barriers came down, people in the service industries were among the first to react—after all, it was the smart move when you wanted to open a man's wallet. It was why bazaar traders in Egypt and Istanbul could greet you in dozens of languages, grinned and said, "Lovely jubbly," whenever they met a Brit and could offer a *"bra pris,"* for a Swede.

Konstantin gave the blackboard menu a cursory glance. He was not particularly hungry, but he needed to eat something, and it was an efficient way to pass the time. He ordered in English.

A few minutes later, a bottle of ice-cold Evian was placed in front of him. He filled his glass, relishing it more than the food when it arrived.

He looked out through the windows, looking for the rest of the nursery—Mossad worked in teams. There was a fourth member of this little nursery around somewhere out there to pick him up as he left. He saw the sudden flame of a cigarette lighter across the road. It was a foolish error for the watcher to make, which in turn made Konstantin question some of the assumptions he had made himself. He had always been led to believe that Mossad were amongst the best trained operatives in the world, which meant that either he was being tailed by someone fresh out of the nursery or...

A car pulled up between the café and his chain-smoking tail.

It was the same model and year as the car that had been waiting over the road from his hotel, but it wasn't the same car. The plates were two digits different. That couldn't have been a coincidence. Two digits different, but still in sequence. Who bought and registered cars in bulk from the same manufacturer? Someone after bulk discount: government agencies. Big corporations. Not intelligence services. And even if they did, spies wouldn't be so stupid as to send identical cars with almost identical registrations out to watch another undercover operative. It was clumsy. It was the kind of thing a spook noticed. That only strengthened Konstantin's suspicions. He was a popular boy.

FIVE

The fire escape creaked.

Orla climbed higher.

The metal groaned under the unfamiliar weight.

There was a light on in the bedroom. She was sure that Konstantin wasn't in his room.

She waited, statue-still, just in case the slightest shifting of her weight would cause another unwelcome groan from the fire escape. She didn't want to tip off whoever was inside his room. She carefully adjusted the rucksack on her back. Everything she needed was in there. She could have left it in the hire car, but that only added an element of chance to the carefully choreographed operation. She didn't want to come back to find it had been stolen by some opportunist thief. The added weight would make the manoeuvre more difficult, but nothing that was easy was worthwhile.

A shadow passed across the window.

It wasn't large enough to be the Russian.

She couldn't make out any more of its owner.

Around the front of the fleapit, she'd made a single-occupant car parked up on the roadside. The driver was twitchy. There was a bag of takeaway food on the passenger seat, suggesting he was in for the long haul. He was watching the hotel door.

The voice in her earpiece guided her every step of the way.

Lethe said wait, so she waited.

The sun hadn't quite set, but the shadow of the neighbouring building masked her in its darkness.

The light went out in the bedroom.

She felt herself relax.

She waited.

She still couldn't move.

Not yet.

She had to be sure that the intruder had left the room and wasn't just lurking in the corridor. Konstantin should have prepped the window for her, but that didn't mean it would open smoothly or soundlessly.

"All clear," came the voice in her ear.

"You sure?" she whispered back. "No surprises waiting?"

"It's traditional for the one coming down the chimney to leave the gifts, not the other way around."

"Funny."

"Fret not, m'dear. No bugs. No scanners. Nothing offering any sort of heat signature or emitting any electronic pulses."

She didn't want to know how he could possibly know that kind of thing. It was enough that he did. She trusted him.

He told her anyway. That was just the way Lethe was: he wanted her to appreciate his genius. "Koni's phone isn't exactly a phone. It's got a few little modifications of my own making. Identifying a transmitter isn't that tricky."

"If you say so."

Orla stretched her muscles, making sure they were warm before clambering from the iron fire escape, swinging across the brickwork, and grasping a handhold in the recess around

Konstantin's window. She drew her leg slowly along the brickwork, feeling for purchase, until she was able to haul herself up into the narrow opening.

The window was closed but unlatched. She could see the holes where nails had been driven into the frame to secure it. There was no sign of the nails themselves. It only took her a couple of seconds to work the window up far enough to wriggle inside.

She settled into the most uncomfortable chair in the room and waited. It was unlikely that Koni's visitor would return; he'd done his job. He'd gone through the Russian's scant belongings and learned everything he was likely to: precisely nothing. At least, nothing that the old man didn't very deliberately intend him to learn.

"Did you get a look at whoever it was that came in?"

"Limited," Lethe said, his voice carrying all the way back from England. "I can't just press point-and-click with government satellites. We're at the mercy of NASA at the moment, and I think we've got about twenty minutes before the orbiting satellite repositions and you're on your own until I can find another one to piggy back."

"You know I love it when you talk geek," Orla said.

"Your man's been driven away in a car that was waiting for him outside."

"I know the one."

"I'm tracking it. No plates. Heading towards the city centre."

"It'd be nice to know whose side he's on." Orla said.

"Gimme a few hours, and I'll know if he prefers boxers or briefs."

"Well, wake me up when you do," she said and pushed herself deeper into the chair.

SIX

She came awake the moment the key scraped into the lock.

She was fully alert by the time the weak light crept into the room from the corridor—a full two seconds before the Russian closed the door. There was a moment when she remembered—vividly—opening her eyes in the hotel bathroom as Sokol pushed her under the water, the kicking and splashing and the sudden fear, but then she realised where she was.

The big man's silhouette diffused most of the light while her eyes adjusted. He closed the door and walked across through the room. She flicked on the bedside lamp.

"The room's clean," Orla said. That didn't stop Konstantin from working it over methodically, checking all of the obvious places where a listening device could have been secreted.

He picked up the mobile phone he had left at the side of the bed. "Checked this yet?"

"Nope," Orla shook her head. "The honour's all yours."

He concentrated on the smartphone's screen, blotting everything else out as he did so.

"Anything?"

"He checked the texts and the address book—"

"So it was worth sending that salacious message to you, eh, big boy?" Orla laughed. The line ironed out some of the creases on Konstantin's face. Not all of them. She'd been given free rein on the texts she sent him under the assumption she was a better flirt than Lethe. It wasn't even close to an imagination-stretcher. The phone she had used was still in England, but Lethe had set up a relay so she could send them from the burner phone, and anyone calling her would be diverted by a backdoor relay to Israel. She wasn't expecting any calls.

"Got the laptop?"

Orla slipped it from her rucksack and fired it up.

She produced a USB cable from her bag and offered one end to Konstantin who connected the phone. Within a minute they were watching video that the equipment had captured while it was being examined.

"Are you getting this, Jude?"

"Running it through facial recognition as we speak. What would you do without me?"

"Not just a pretty voice, eh?"

Konstantin opened his bag on the bed, checking its contents.

"Anything missing?" Orla asked him.

The Russian shook his head, running a penlight over it. The blue-light would have revealed the presence of new prints if there'd been any to find. Their uninvited guest had been wearing gloves. "No. But the bag's been checked and repacked. Everything's in the same order, folded in exactly the same way, right down to the mis-folded corner—so they were methodical."

"They didn't want you knowing you'd had visitors."

It did not surprise her in the slightest.

The Israelis wouldn't be against Konstantin doing their dirty work. It was deniable, and that deniability kept their hands clean, while business still got taken care of. It was the classic win-win as far as they were concerned—as long as they could keep an eye on him. Most governments were surprisingly happy to have deniable crews operate black-bag jobs when it came to sensitive operations. And this, quite literally, was a black-bag job.

Orla packed away the laptop.

The phone had yielded all the useful information it was likely to.

All they could do now was wait.

Konstantin reached down to the bottom of his black bag to retrieve his Glock. He had left it there deliberately for his visitor to find. Mossad expected him to have a weapon. They wouldn't expect him to go into Palestine unarmed. The plan was that they wouldn't suspect he'd brought a second piece into the country. He handed Orla the second gun, a Jericho 941, weapon of choice for the Israeli Defence Force, along with the box of ammunition. It was also Orla's favourite handgun: effective without being showy, and more than capable of putting the enemy down from distance. She would never have been able to bring it into the country on a commercial airline, and tracking down a weapon for her on site would have wasted more time than they had.

"Thanks," she said, checking the weapon. The clip was full. She tucked it into the waistband of her jeans. There was no need to say any more; they each knew what was expected of the other. They would make their way separately into Palestine.

"Got him," Lethe said in Orla's ear said.

She glanced at Konstantin.

"Surprise me," she said.

"Yossi Mordecai, IDF. Enough in his personnel file to suggest he's Mossad."

Good, bad or indifferent, it brought a level of certainty to what was going on.

"What about the team from the café?" Konstantin asked, pressing a finger to his earpiece. It was small and unobtrusive, barely visible unless you were looking for it.

"Nothing."

"Team?" Orla asked. "You were followed?"

"Team of three inside the café, posing as students. Chain-smoker lurking outside. The team inside were proficient. Smoker not particularly skilled. Unless he was deliberately trying to be made."

"So someone else knows you are here."

"Three cannot keep a secret," Konstantin said, meaning Mossad wasn't watertight.

It was certainly possible.

There were elements within the security agency that would be against an outsider coming in and acting on land they considered theirs by right. It was their job to maintain security; their job to protect their own people; their job to deal with enemies of the state, no one else's. If Konstantin failed, then they would be given the green light to take care of business.

And what better way to make sure that he failed than to tip off the Palestinians?

Play one off against the other, and then stand well back to watch the fireworks.

"Next move?" Orla asked.

"Sit tight for a day, then make it clear that I know that my cover has been compromised," Konstantin said. "They won't do anything as long as I'm on Israeli soil. The old man can pull me out of here and make it known that they've got a leak. As long as they are watching me, they won't be looking for you."

He was right.

SEVEN

It was still dark when Orla slipped out through the bedroom window.

She had managed to grab a few hours' sleep.

That would have to be enough for now.

There would be few people crossing into Palestine at first light. The flow of bodies would be greater in the other direction. The security checkpoints were there to protect the people of Israel, not the other way around. She had a cover in place: the address of a family scribbled on a much-folded piece of paper, the name of a relative she was supposed to be visiting. It wouldn't stand up to any serious scrutiny; the house in question was rubble.

She'd taken the opportunity to shower and put on fresh clothes before leaving, but that first freshness was already gone. The heat of the day had done it, and the dust that was being kicked up as migrant Palestinian workers passed slowly through the gate into Jerusalem. She had her passport at the ready, expecting it to be thoroughly scrutinised by the machine-gun-wielding guard standing by the sentry house. He waved her through with the slightest of nods. There was something about the way he looked at her. It took her a moment to realise he was mentally undressing her; it was a small price to pay.

The laptop weighed down on her back. She wondered if it was worth keeping, or if she should just discard it. There was nothing sensitive on it. She could have left it with Konstantin; even if his 'eyes' had made a second visit and stumbled across it, they would have assumed he'd had it with him when they checked his room before. She didn't need it. She could send and receive data via the uplink from her smartphone. But there were advantages to carrying the machine. It was far more powerful than her phone, for a start. And it offered an element of secrecy from the IDF, as it wasn't permanently connected to their 3G networks and telecommunication satellites. She suspected that might come in useful before the day was out.

She'd copied the photographs of the target onto her phone.

She didn't anticipate having to reference them; she would be able to pick the man out of a crowd. Even without him, the mere presence of his number two would make her flesh creep the moment he came within fifty yards of her.

Flashbacks surged through her like a series of bitter electric shocks, each one churning her stomach more than the last.

Orla had dared to think she was over it; she was wrong.

She wasn't even close to being over it.

For the first time, she wondered if she was up to the job.

Too late now, she thought bitterly. She could only hope that successfully wrapping the job up would offer some kind of closure.

Bile rose in her throat as she stepped onto Palestinian soil.

Part of her just wanted to crumple to the ground, but she couldn't afford to do that. The guard was still admiring her arse as she walked away.

It wasn't until she was masked by a queue of people waiting to cross over in the other direction that Orla allowed herself a moment to gather herself. She rested against a wall. A couple of the younger men in the line turned to look at her. She had seen the look before in some Middle Eastern countries: disdain. It was a look that said that the way she dressed made her a whore in their eyes. The cotton cut-offs and T-shirt she wore were conservative compared to anything they would have encountered in London, but that only proved how damned the West was.

One woman began to step out of the line, but the man beside her caught her elbow and kept her walking.

Orla reached in her bag for a bottle of water.

She took a deep swallow from it. It was still refreshing, even if it was warm. She rinsed the acid from her mouth and spat it out against the wall. That earned her more disapproval from the slowly shuffling queue. She poured some of the water onto her handkerchief. She wiped her face and the back of her neck with it, and then tied the wet cloth around her forehead like a bandana.

The moment had passed.

She felt ready to face the world—or at least this part of it.

She walked on, aiming for the shadow between two houses further up the dusty road. She retrieved the earpiece from the hidden pouch in her rucksack as she stowed the water bottle, and slipped it into place. She thumbed down the button, powering it up.

"You there, handsome?" she asked.

"Gotcha, gorgeous," came Jude's reply. There was a slight lag. "Made it through okay?"

"No problems. You got the latest for me?"

"Sending it to your phone now. Any idea of how you're going to make contact?"

"Not yet."

"Ah, the classic wing-it stratagem. I think the old man's going to want something a little more concrete than that."

"Is he listening in?"

"Nope. Still flat out in the Land of Nod."

Orla checked her watch. Jerusalem was only a couple of hours ahead of the UK, and the Land of Nod was the territory outside of Eden that Adam and Eve were banished to after the whole forbidden fruit affair. She could well imagine Lethe had been up half of the night thinking of that reference. It certainly wouldn't be the first time that he'd set up a camp bed in that room for the duration of an operation.

Her phone vibrated, signalling receipt of an incoming email.

She scrolled through satellite images of the Jenin encampment in the Hawashin district, along with co-ordinates.

"Well then, if he's asleep, I'll leave it to you to be creative. Try not to make him worry."

"Thanks. Shouldn't you be walking? It's eight miles to the camp. You really don't want to be out in the full heat of the day."

"I don't want to do it at all," she said to herself.

EIGHT

Frost stood back as the man pushed the door open.

The building had been badly damaged in the bombings that had taken place during the downfall of Qaḏḏāfi's regime. Most of the upper floor had been reduced to rubble and a couple of exterior walls. A corner of the roof perched precariously in place. A heavy storm would bring the whole thing crashing to the ground. The only reason it was still standing was that it didn't rain much in this part of the world.

As they walked through the back alleys, he spotted spent shells in the rubble; they told a very vivid story of the street fighting and the recent revolution.

A man stepped inside—more tentatively than Frost would have liked—and shouted something in Arabic. Frost had a smattering of the language, but he couldn't make out more than a few syllables. The man spoke far too quickly.

"Perhaps he is on the telephone," the black-marketeer said, explaining the seeming rudeness of their host. "His door would be tightly locked if he was not open for business. He keeps many valuables here."

It was hard to imagine anyone keeping anything of value in a place like this.

If it were secure, then it was because people were afraid of the man, or the people he represented.

When a regime fell, there were always people who would step in to fill the vacuum and exploit any and every opportunity they could before the new government was fully established. It was the same the world over. The only question was whether it would be locals taking advantage of the situation, or some large corporation getting into the 'new markets' before their competitors could. It came dressed in pretty clothes—they would tender for contracts to rebuild the infrastructure—but basically, it came down to them being paid to put back up the stuff they'd helped tear down.

Frost took a quick glance up and down the alley to see if any unwelcome eyes were lurking in any of the doorways. He was naturally cautious; it kept him alive. Going into unknown and possibly hostile territory with his back exposed wasn't smart. The street was empty.

But something still felt wrong.

He wasn't a big believer in sixth sense or any of that nonsense, but something felt *wrong* here.

"This way, this way," the man beckoned, urging him to follow. Frost could tell that he was nervous he was about to lose him—and the slice of cash his 'finders fee' would earn him.

Frost followed him past a flight of stairs. The stairs led to an upstairs that wasn't there anymore. Frost followed him along a short corridor lit only by a single, naked bulb. The bulb was too dim to reveal the state of the ceiling. He saw a ragged line of bullet holes in the plaster.

It was surprising that there was still electricity reaching the building.

The man paused at another door, this one slightly ajar.

He tapped, and called again.

Silence.

The black-marketeer pushed tentatively at the door.

It swung in slowly.

"Mister Nasri?"

Nasri? The name meant nothing to Frost, but it was something for Lethe to play with. His companion stepped inside, but then spoke so rapidly that Frost had no hope of understanding. The only two syllables he recognised were the name Allah. The black-marketeer pushed by him in a hurry to get out of the room. Frost watched him run toward the main door.

He didn't follow him.

He didn't have to step into the room to see the dead man.

The blood was long dried.

Flies buzzed around the body.

They'd already started laying their eggs. Given the heat and the stench, it was obvious they were beginning to hatch. The man lay between the door and the desk. Reading the scene, Frost decided that simple fact meant it was unlikely the body belonged to Nasri.

Frost paused for a moment, listening.

If someone had been watching, the Arab's distress would have tipped him or her off that the body had been found. No one came running.

He crouched down beside the body.

Rats had gnawed on the soft tissue.

He was used to death, and had seen much worse than this.

The dead man had been shot twice: once in the chest, and once in the head. The first shot, to the chest, had killed him. The second served one purpose: to make it hard to identify him. It was unlikely there would be a significant database of fingerprints or dental records to draw upon. A man without a face could present significant difficulties for the authorities, assuming that they were interested in trying to identify him.

Frost turned the corpse over.

A handful of maggots slipped from the open wound and onto the carpet.

He suspected that he'd found the missing Kasim, but there was no way of being sure. He fished his phone from his pocket and took several photographs of the man's ruined face from different angles. There was facial reconstruction software—he didn't know how it worked, or even *if* it worked, but if there was a chance Lethe could put Humpty back together again, they had to give it a shot.

The safe door hung open.

The interior was empty; if Nasri kept valuables here, their absence was a good indication the man was long gone and not coming back. It was not hard to put two and two together. Frost hoped that he was coming up with four. Kasim had brought the ring to Nasri looking for a fair price, only to pay with his life.

"Lethe?" There was a delay before he received a response. He caught the trailing edge of another conversation; Lethe was relaying Intel to Orla.

By nature, the team were all loners, but they functioned as a unit because Lethe was the glue that held them all together.

"Come in, Frosty," Lethe said a moment later.

"I think I've found our thief."

"Good work, that, man. So, what does he have to say for himself?"

Frost glanced at the dead man. "Given the bullet holes, not very much." There was silence at the other end and Frost felt the need to add to his statement. "Nothing to do with me. He's been dead for several days."

"Right."

"Yeah, the guy has been shot in the face, point-blank. I'm sending you a picture now. Not sure if there's enough left for a positive ID."

"Let me worry about that."

"I've got a number for you, need to know the last number dialled."

"Why not just hit redial?"

"If I said it was an old style Bakelite phone, would that mean anything to you?"

"Give me the number. It may take a while."

"I've also got a name. Nasri. Black-market artefact trader. I think he's our shooter, and most likely in possession of the Seal."

"Assuming Nasri is his real name."

Frost took another look around the room.

He didn't want to leave until he was sure that he'd considered every possibility, every angle.

There was nothing of interest in the desk drawers.

The metal waste paper basked contained only ash and black fragments of paper.

The man may have left in a hurry, but he'd had the presence of mind to destroy anything incriminating. He checked the remains in the bin. They crumbled to dust at the slightest of touches.

There was a commotion outside.

"Time to go," Frost said, as much to himself as Lethe.

It could be the authorities; associates of Nasri come to clean up the mess, or another unknown hostile. It really didn't matter which: he didn't intend to stick around to find out.

He checked the window.

It was barred.

He checked the corridor.

It was still empty.

But the noise from outside increased.

They were getting nearer.

The only way was up t

he broken staircase.

He didn't hesitate. He ran for the stairs, taking the steps two at a time.

His footsteps echoed loudly.

Frost slowed down, knowing the noise could give him away.

The stairs turned through a-hundred-and-eighty degrees by the time he reached the first landing. Down below, the new arrivals entered the building.

Frost held his breath and stood motionless.

"Everything okay there, Frosty?" Lethe's voice came in his ear, louder than his heartbeat. He couldn't silence him for fear someone would hear him. Lethe didn't say anything else. The procedure was ingrained. Radio silence until the man on the ground checked in.

From his hiding place in the shadows, Frost watched as a group of men—including the black-marketeer who'd brought him—made their way towards the room and the dead man inside it. That answered one question: another man remained in the doorway. He was solid—big enough to blot out most of the sunlight that had been creeping in through it. There was no easy way out. He had two options: stay where he was and wait it out, or continue up. The longer he waited where he was, the greater the chances of discovery. He would have to tread softly because of the rubble on the stairs.

There wouldn't be anything worthwhile up there—looters would have removed anything salvageable long ago.

He didn't care about that.

All he needed was a way out.

Every step increased the risk of discovery.

It felt as if it took forever to climb the ten steps to the next landing.

The voices downstairs grew louder as the men argued amongst themselves. He couldn't make out the actual words, but it didn't take a genius to know they were arguing about what they should do about the body. In a place like this, there were as many ways to dispose of a corpse, as there were to make one.

Frost leaned against the wall at the top of the stairs.

He regretted it the moment he did.

The wall moved against his weight. It sent crumbling rubble onto the staircase. The sudden movement and noise caused a bird to shoot up from it nest in one of the cool shadowy crevices, startling Frost. He took another step back, involuntarily, as its wings flapped at his face.

A voice came from below: the big man in the doorway. He couldn't have missed the scuffle of footsteps, rubble and wings.

"Bollocks," Frost grunted.

Heavy footsteps came up the stairway, moving cautiously.

Frost knew he'd be moving with his back pressed against the wall, gun in hand. He had to get out of here, fast.

"I need an evac route. Now."

"Ready to jump?"

"Better than getting pumped full of lead."

"Okay. You see the remains of an interior wall standing in the middle of the building? Get yourself to it. Then run straight to the far end of the building and jump. The wall should shield you. And I mean *jump,* Frosty. There are iron railings or something down there you've got to clear. Run fast, jump far, and with a little bit of luck, you'll break your fall on the roof of a transit van."

He didn't need to ask if this was the best chance he'd got—he trusted Lethe. If this was it, this really was *it*. Thinking twice just wasted precious time.

And the ricochet of the first bullet slamming into concrete, far too close for comfort, was more than enough to convince him it was time to learn to fly. The man emerged from the stairwell just as he made it to the cover of the retaining wall.

The Arab shouted—it could have been a polite request to stop; it could have been an order to put his hands up, bend over and prepare to kiss his arse goodbye. It didn't make a blind bit of difference to Frost. He ignored it.

He ducked behind the wall.

A bullet tore through the plaster a few inches from his head.

So much for a safe place.

He started to run.

"Faster," Lethe yelled in his earpiece.

Frost gritted his teeth and launched himself into the air, kicking out, legs cycling desperately. He caught a glimpse of the spikes on top of the iron railings, and then the fact that the van was already moving registered. He was screwed. There was no way he was going to hit the roof if it peeled away from the curb. He closed his eyes only to open them again at the jarring impact of the roof under his backside. The movement of the van and the momentum of his wild jump carried him off the top and slammed him into the wall of the neighbouring building.

Frost tried to grab onto the van before he went over the side but there was nothing to grab onto. All he could do was go with it.

A bullet hit the van.

The driver did not stop.

He floored it, tyres screeching as he roared down the street. Another gunshot rang out.

The sound of shots didn't bring any gawkers.

The uprising wasn't so long ago; people kept their heads down when they heard shots.

For once, luck was on his side. He came off the roof and landed painfully in a pile of rubble from another of the buildings that had come down. He lay there waiting, jagged edges of brick digging into his spine, hoping the gunman thought he'd ridden out of there on the roof of the van.

A moment later he heard a car engine roar into life, tyres spitting gravel and dust as a Mercedes set off after the van.

Frost didn't move until he was sure no one was watching.

"Silky smooth," Lethe said in his ear.

NINE

Orla followed the directions using the GPS function on her phone.

The lurking fear had faded to a general discomfort.

She had a job to do, and she would do it to the best of her ability.

If she needed a break she would take it—but only after this was over. For now, she had to be all-in. People were relying on her to complete her part of the operation.

The news that Frost had turned up a lead meant that they had something to follow. It didn't mean that they had any better idea of where the Seal was. They couldn't be sure if it had even left Libya. It was down to Lethe now, and whether he could trace anything on the back channels and bulletin boards and private sub-ether networks he haunted. If it were being talked about, he'd find it. If they weren't talking about it, well, Lethe was good, but even he needed a little time to do the impossible.

A street vendor sold lemonade in chipped bottles from a rickety table.

Orla stopped to take a drink; it was barely mid-morning, but the heat was already unbearable. She'd forgotten just how bad it could be.

Lethe's voice sounded in her ear.

She couldn't respond without looking very strange in front of the lemonade man. He'd remember unusual behaviour—and a woman talking to herself was unusual enough for him to remember exactly what she looked like.

She swallowed the last of the lemonade, the sting of the acid burning the back of her throat. She smiled as she handed back the glass bottle. He gave her a toothless smile in return. She turned her back on him and walked a few steps away before she confirmed she was listening.

"Okay guys, everyone's here, so here's what we've got. Our man goes by the name of Iqbal Nasri. He's an integral part of the growing criminal fraternity that has sprung up now that there's no one to slap them down. He has dual nationality, and is currently travelling on his French passport."

"Travelling?" It was Konstantin.

"Yep. He's mobile. Left Libya two days ago for Rome. He's booked on a flight from Rome to Jerusalem at 16:00 today. We're ahead of the game for the first time. We know where he's going to be."

"Why Rome?" Noah asked.

"Sir Charles suspects Nasri may have attempted to sell the ring to the Vatican."

"No shit? Well, that's ambitious," Noah said.

"Despite the global double-dip recession, it's not as though the Catholics are exactly short of a bob or two," said Frost.

"True, but they aren't the only ones with disposable income," Lethe said.

"You reckon the Palestinians can outbid them?" Noah said. "Hard to imagine. I would have thought that the Israelis would have been better placed to buy it."

"It's not always about money," Lethe said. "Nasri is a devout Muslim. Selling to the Jews or the Catholics would go against his faith."

"Unless money is his true religion?" Noah offered.

"Unlikely, given the names of some of his known associates."

"I would have thought there'd be plenty of Middle Eastern interest," Orla said after glancing around briefly to make sure that she wasn't overheard.

"That's where it gets a little more interesting," Lethe said, and then fell silent. Orla knew that he was enjoying himself. When none of them asked him to go on, he sighed. "You take all the fun out of this, you know?" he said eventually.

"Not for us," Orla said.

"Fine. Nasri's sister is married to Saddiq. I'll just let that sink in for a moment," Lethe said.

Orla certainly hadn't expected that kind of connection.

When they finally responded, they all spoke at once.

Orla did not try to compete with Frost's more forceful voice. They'd all ask the same questions anyway.

Sir Charles' voice broke through the chatter. "Nasri is a dangerous man. Saddiq is military—brutal with his own men, and quite prepared to show no mercy to his enemies—but Nasri is sadistic. Kasim Hamid got off lightly."

"Frost, Larkin, that will be all, gentlemen. Orla, Konstantin, we've had word from Control. We seem to have crossed into an on-going investigation and the Israelis want to use Konstantin to confirm certain Intel that has come into their possession."

"Go on," said the Russian.

"Saddiq has taken shelter in the ruins of the Jenin refugee camp."

Orla didn't say anything.

What she didn't say was that was where she'd finally wished once and for all that she were dead. What she didn't say was that was where the Beast had brutally raped and abused her.

Konstantin knew some of it. Sir Charles knew all of it.

What was the point of repeating it?

"It was suggested by Control that you might not be up for it, and they want to pull you out," the old man said. "I'm not happy about it, but I agreed to give you the choice. Konstantin can do this alone if he has to. So, knowing where Saddiq is, and what it means to you personally, dear girl, what do you want to do?"

"Nothing's changed," Orla said.

"Do not take any unnecessary risks. Konstantin, you're Orla's shadow. The Israelis know you are there, so don't make contact, but for Christ's sake, make sure no harm comes to her. Okay?"

"Understood," the Russian said.

"Peachy," Orla said.

It was anything but.

TEN

The last time she was here:

She lay in near darkness.

Moonlight tried to creep in through the tiny window high in the wall; it was smaller than her hand, so even without the bars there would be no escape.

The air was filled with the odour of sweat, of bodily waste, and sex.

She dreaded the moment when the darkness would break again, because she knew what came with the light. It wasn't relief. It wasn't hope. It had happened too many times for her to fool herself now.

Orla tried to concentrate on the pain.

The pain gave her a reason to be angry.

It was better to fixate on the anger than be torn apart by the fear.

She drew her knees tighter to her chest.

She wrapped her arms around them and pressed her back against the cold plaster-daub wall.

She heard them coming and going outside. Voices hushed in conversation. Laughter.

The door opened.

One of the men stood silhouetted in the doorway.

He brought pain with him.

"Unsurprisingly, your government disavows all knowledge of your entry into Palestine. Sensibly, they do not deny that you are employed by them, but in this instance they assure us you are not here on their business."

"It's true," she lied, the swelling of her bottom lip made simple words uncomfortable. She had known that they would deny any knowledge of her; admitting sending her in would send up warning flares two miles high. "I'm sightseeing."

"That is unfortunate," he said. It sounded like he actually meant it. "The British Government will not deal with terrorists or kidnappers. They have abandoned you."

It was true. Even if she'd been an ordinary citizen, the Powers That Be would have been prepared for the worst case scenario and let her die rather than give into the demands of Islamic Jihadists.

They didn't bargain. That meant her only way out lay in getting word out to the IDF that the men they wanted were here, signalling the tanks to roll in. She couldn't pull a disappearing act.

She said nothing. There was nothing she could say that would make things any better.

"We do not believe them. We think they are looking to save some money. Perhaps they hope to get you for a discount. Forty per cent off, every spy must go? Is that how your government works? Or do they really not value your life?"

"If they say they won't pay, they won't pay," she said.

The man leaned forward and she could smell his hot, foetid breath as she had too many times before. She knew each of them by their stink, even in the darkness.

It was rare that any light made it into the room, and even then, she caught no more than a glimpse of their faces: a part of the cheek, the side of a brow, a dark eye. But she had seen this one when they had made the proof of life video.

In the most general terms, not being able to identify your kidnappers increased the chances of release, but not by much.

Right now she was alive—and that was all she cared about.

That would change, though.

There would come a point where the brutality of her captors, the waterboarding, the electro shocks, the battering, and at the end of it, stripped, beaten and gang raped by faceless men in the dark, being alive would become the problem, not the end-game. An hour ago they had threatened to blind her with a heated spoon. She didn't know how long it would take for her to reach the tipping point; she was stronger than they thought, though.

She had to be.

"Tell them you need to talk to Sir Charles Wyndham. He will pay," she said. She hoped they bought it. All she wanted to do was get a message to the old man, let Lethe decipher the exact location of her prison, let Koni come bursting through that door, let Noah gather her up into his arms and carry her out of there like the broken hero he always wanted to be... But for that, she had to stay alive. They wanted money, and the mere mention of a title, a Sir, meant money to them. And to get money, they needed to sit her in front of a camera and make her plead. So for now, at least, greed would keep her alive.

But it wouldn't keep her safe from the kind of sick bastards who thought rape was the worst thing they could do to a woman.

He came closer.

She tried to turn her face away.

He caught her head and kept it still.

His thumb pressed into the tenderness on the side of her mouth. She could feel the rough calluses.

He breathed in deeply through his nose, leaning in close to savour her smell. It had been far too long since she'd been able to shower. She tried to move her head but his grip was unrelenting. His tongue licked the side of her face. This was the least of the things they had done to her—and by rights should have been easier to endure than the rape. But it wasn't. The violations had merged, now they were one continuous abuse.

The first man they had sent in to rape her had almost been reluctant—hesitant, if not gentle—but this man had been there, standing in the doorway, mocking him, telling him to hurt her, to punish her, use her like a pig, make her squeal and beg, piss on her, grab her hair and choke her. He wouldn't do it.

But that was only the first time.

Since then, he had come back.

Twice he had been on his own. More times he had been with others. Alone, he was never rough; with others, he was a vicious bastard.

Her instinct had been to resist, to fight, but they wanted her to do that, and fighting only made it worse. It escalated the violence. So she didn't fight it. Survival. That was all that mattered. They would come for her. All she had to do was stay alive—at any cost.

The time would come when one of them would want her dead; she needed allies in here.

This one enjoyed causing pain too much. That worried her.

She had given them names. The names reflected how she saw them, and served to make the monsters more human. Apart from this one. He was the Beast: all anger and rage bubbling under the surface, ready to erupt at the slightest provocation.

She needed to watch herself around the Beast. One wrong word could set him off.

Then there was the one she thought of as the Boy—still raw enough to be moulded, perhaps even manipulated into quiet rebellion. He wore a Greenpeace badge on his jacket, which gave her hope. It was an unlikely cause to find here in Hell, but maybe it meant he was capable of believing in something beyond Jihad?

They had talked about it once, in the stillness of the night.

He confessed that he had been to university in England, sent by his family to help make a better life for them here in Palestine. Like so many dreams, it had come to nothing.

She liked the Boy—if like was the right word, given the context of their 'friendship'—but there was no room for sentiment. If it came down to it, he was an easy sacrifice.

"A new name? Does this one have money?" the Beast said. "Because if I don't get my money there will be… consequences. I will make you regret becoming a spy."

"I'm not a—" she started to say, but then his hand moved, grabbing a fistful of hair and snapping her head back.

"Did I say you could speak? Did I? Do you know how sick I am of hearing your voice?"

She didn't say anything.

She didn't move.

If he saw anything approaching fear in her eyes that would only serve to drive the Beast on.

He gripped her hair tighter, tearing out a handful as he yanked her head back.

When she looked at him again there was a tear in the corner of her eye.

He smiled.

A gap-toothed smile of victory.

He raised his free hand.

Orla braced herself for the pain.

But the pain didn't arrive.

ELEVEN

Konstantin threw the paperback at the wall in frustration.

There were times when he thought about paying these peddlers of make-believe a night time visit, turning up on their doorsteps at three a.m. and showing them that it wasn't all 'heat of battle', giving them a glimpse of what it was really like to take a life, to draw a knife across someone's throat, feel a bullet tear through muscle and shatter bone.

They had no idea.

It didn't even help to kill time.

Boredom: the worst enemy of the active man.

There was only so much of it he could take.

Even just walking around the city would have felt like he was doing something.

It had been hours since they'd lost contact with Orla.

That was a lifetime.

She'd gone dark before she'd crossed the border. The old man had told him to protect her, and now all he was doing was chasing shadows. He didn't like it. But she was a big girl. She knew what she was doing. He had to trust her. But that wasn't easy. Not here. Not in this place. Not when it came loaded with the baggage of her past life. He was half-tempted to slip the Glock into the waistband of his jeans and stride into Hell like some comic book hero.

But he could hardly do that and keep a low profile. No, he needed a plan.

It didn't help that his tail seemed intent to stick around like a dose of herpes. He felt like crossing the street to confront the cigarette smoking man and just say, "Look, I think my partner's in trouble in there, I need your people." But that wouldn't have gone down well with the Powers That Be. And if Orla was fine, and this bad feeling of his was nothing more than that—a bad feeling—he'd be jeopardising everything for nothing. He had to trust her. She *would* be okay.

He stood in the window, looking down at the street.

The cigarette smoker leant against the side of a building over the way. He'd moved less than fifty yards from his previous spot. The relocation was more about comfort than camouflage. The man wasn't hiding. His plan hinged on the watchers thinking they'd interfered just enough for the Russian to abort.

Konstantin left the room.

The only things he took with him were the Glock, his phone, and the comlink.

The chain smoker kept his distance as Konstantin made his way towards the shopping district. They wouldn't search his room again, but just in case they decided to be anal about it, he decided to amuse himself. He'd marked out odd words in the paperback that spelt out a message, making it appear that he'd received coded orders to abort.

"Can you hear me, big man?" Lethe's voice buzzed in his ear like one of the flies picking over the carcass of Jerusalem. Even over the sound of traffic—which was building up as he moved closer to the city centre—Konstantin could still hear him loud and clear.

"Go."

"Nasri's plane touched down your end about ten minutes ago. Control had pulled strings and grounded the original flight from Rome, but they couldn't keep every plane on the hardstand for days, so Nasri had managed to get himself on the next flight, losing a few hours. Sorry it couldn't have been more. Frosty'll be with you in another hour. The old man wants you to tail Nasri from the airport until Frost can take over while you go in after Orla."

"Difficult with my chain smoking shadow."

"You're a big ugly boy, Koni; lose him. They can't know you're tailing Nasri, or the whole thing falls apart."

"And if I lose my smoker, they'll know something's up. They are going to get itchy."

"Then give them something to scratch, Koni. Use your initiative. You're a devious bastard. Make it look like it was his fault that he lost you, rather than the other way around."

"I could just take him out. Hide the body. It would be days before they found him."

"No," Sir Charles interrupted.

Konstantin hated it when the old man did that; listening in. "Hello, boss," he said.

"Konstantin."

"If I can't kill him, what do you suggest?"

"That's completely up to you, but don't make a mess. We don't want the eyes of Israel and Palestine staring at us. Make him fail. How you do it us up to you. They cannot know we are monitoring Nasri."

"Any word from Orla?"

"No."

"I'm not happy about any of this. She's in there alone. You know what happened to her there before," the Russian said. The inference was clear. He would trigger an all-out war if he had to, but he was getting her out of there.

"I do." Sir Charles said. "Hand Nasri over to Frost, then go find her."

Go find her.

It would have been so much more satisfying to make the enemy hurt first, but he couldn't afford to play games.

He had an idea how he could ditch his shadow without drawing too much attention to himself. As ideas went, it was not one of his better ones. But it was effective, and that was all that mattered.

There were places in the city he could go to that the Arab wouldn't be able to follow. It wasn't perfect, but if he decided to pay a visit to a synagogue, the chain smoker would just wait outside patiently and pick him up as he left.

There was an alternative, though, and it was very much a 'Noah Larkin' sort of idea. He doubted the old man would have approved.

There were places like this in almost every city in the world: where the lights were red, the streets were walked, and the professionals were amongst the oldest in the world. The way to find what you were looking for was to ask a taxi driver. They knew everything, especially when it came to the seedier side of things.

He needed to give his tail just long enough to get mobile. That could be the hardest part. If he hailed a passing cab, there was a good chance he'd leave the man behind too quickly. He needed a taxi rank with a queue. He needed the queue to be sure it would take a while for him to get into the cab. The chain smoker needed to call his wheels around into a position he could maintain eyes on Konstantin at all times.

It took a little while, but he found one.

While Konstantin waited in line, a car pulled up just a short distance away. He used a reflection in a coffee shop window to confirm that it was the same car he had seen the day before.

Finally he reached the front of the line. He climbed into the back of the taxi.

"American?" the driver asked, though it was clear that English was not his first language. Konstantin didn't want to disappoint the man, and put on his best John Wayne drawl.

"You betcha."

"So where to, buddy?"

"I'm looking for a little company, if you know what I mean?"

The man glanced over his shoulder with a grin on his face. "Ah, looking for a good time? What kind of girl you looking for? You like them young enough to bleed, Yankee? I know where you can get a nice young girl if that's your kind of thing?"

Konstantin clenched his fist, struggling to keep the tourist-smile in place.

If he got *anywhere* near a place like that, the only blood would be from the Johns and the bastards peddling kids. "Not my kind of thing."

"Okay, okay, how about I take you to a nice place? Clean girls, clean sheets? But dirty, dirty minds."

That sounded better. Konstantin nodded his approval. "Is it far?"

"Ten minutes. Maybe a little longer in this traffic."

"If I think you're giving me the tour just to run your clock up, I'll know. And I won't like it. Neither will you."

The driver clicked the counter off. "Ah, my friend. I wouldn't do that to you. We're buddies. Special price: Twenty dollars American, how's that sound, buddy?"

"Sure thing," Konstantin said, knowing that he was overpaying, but that by agreeing, he would be taken directly there, and the driver would feel that he had done well out of the fare, too. It was sound in theory. The driver would be less likely to remember him if he didn't give him reason to. The mind was like that. It started to accumulate details when it was given anchor-points to remember. Remember the tourist who wanted to get laid and argued about the price of the fare, and you'd be able to remember he was a big guy, you'd remember the intense stare and the plastered-on smile, and slowly, you'd begin to bring back other details. He didn't want that.

In less than five minutes, they were outside what appeared to be a small hotel.

There was nothing on the outside to mark it out as a brothel.

The driver got out of the taxi and led the way in. It wasn't personal service; the guy was making sure he got his cut for bringing them a client.

Konstantin glanced up the street and sure enough, there was the chain smoker, puffing away beside the driver.

Konstantin assumed they'd know what this place was; and if they didn't, they'd radio it in and someone would tell them. They'd expect to have to wait, maybe an hour, possibly two, giving him time to shower and clean the whore off his skin.

Two hours was more than enough time for him to disappear.

TWELVE

The last time she was here:

Another sunrise; another sleepless night.

It was an endless cycle.

Orla was a soldier. She tried to grab moments of sleep whenever she could, but this wasn't a normal war. This was her own personal hell. The only sounds she heard were those of her captors moving around. She heard them shouting to each other in Arabic. Every now and again, she caught a snatch of laughter. That was the worst sound. She didn't want to listen to them enjoying themselves, because she didn't want to think about what was amusing them. The Beast's voice always drew the loudest laugh. She told herself that she never heard Boy joining in. She didn't know if that was true or not. It didn't really matter if it was; she only needed to believe it for hope to burn on. Someone would come. They wouldn't leave her here like this.

She scoured every inch of the cell, looking for anything that could be used as a weapon, anything that could be used to help her escape.

There wasn't so much as a scrap of metal in the dirty mattress she lay on. No twisted springs. Nothing. Everything that was brought in with her meals was accounted for when the empty plates were taken away. If she shouted and screamed, her hands and ankles were tied and her mouth gagged.

Silence was golden, in more ways than one, especially when it came to the Beast's satisfaction. He enjoyed her pain. Silence denied him pleasure.

She needed her hands free, no matter what it cost her.

She had a plan.

She wouldn't die here.

The door opened again.

The Boy must have been able to hear her holding her breath from the doorway, because he seemed uneasy. Hesitant. He watched her huddled up against the wall. He had a bowl in his hands. He stepped inside without saying a word. It could have been a shadow, it could have been a bruise, but there was dark shading along his jawline. The Beast's handiwork? Maybe the Boy had tried to stand up to him. If he had, then she might not have that much time left.

He couldn't look her in the eye. That wasn't a good sign.

Orla accepted the bowl from him gratefully. He gave her a bottle of warm water he pulled from his pocket.

She drank thirstily.

He sat in silence, half turned away from her.

"You okay?" she asked, putting the bowl down on the floor.

"They are going to kill you," he said.

She said nothing. She'd known it was coming.

"Two days. If they don't get the money they will kill you. They're not going to get the money, are they?"

She shook her head.

She was dead—it was only a matter of her death catching up with her.

"It's not your fault," she said, breaking the silence.

"That doesn't make it any better. I tried to get them to just let you go," he shrugged, looking even more like a little boy playing at being an adult. "They said that would make us look weak. Killing you sends a message: we are not weak. Next time, they will pay."

"They won't," she said.

"I know that."

"So why? Why are you doing this?" And before he could say money, she said, "What's the money for?" She had nothing to lose by asking, and now that he was resigned to her death, there was more chance of him telling her. It couldn't be about personal gain. Terrorism, no matter what form it took, was never about the accumulation of personal wealth. That wasn't in the psychology of terror.

"We have to make people listen," he said. It sounded so naïve, so optimistic when he said it, like he really believed the world would listen just because they killed her. "We have a right to this land. Just because a guilty world wanted to put things right for the Jews after the war, doesn't mean that we should suffer. They were given our land. Our land. And they keep taking more, even when the rest of the world tells them to stop. No one will stand up to them. So we have to."

"Is this some kind of religious thing, then?"

"No. There are enough who hate the Zionists for their beliefs, or at least use that as the reason for their hatred. We just want them to leave us alone. They think that our rights are of little consequence compared to their own suffering."

Orla waited, hoping that there was more to come.

There was, but not words, only tears.

She saw what she was looking for: a metal badge on his jacket. It wasn't much to gamble your life on. A Greenpeace badge.

Greenpeace were just another one of 'those' organisations, as far as she was concerned. The world needed groups like them, CND, and the like; groups that showed people still cared about something. As long as it still cared, phrases like Broken Britain were nothing but neat little descriptors dreamed up by journalists. As long as people still cared, there was a chance the world wouldn't go to shit. But this was more than just a badge. It was the nearest thing to a weapon she could get her hands on. But a badge, against all of those guns out there? Well, it was hardly a fair fight. Orla could disable the Boy if she had to, but it wouldn't do her any good. She had to even up the odds somehow.

She raised a hand to his cheek. It was a tender gesture. She wiped a tear away with her thumb.

He winced at her touch.

Orla could understand the pain he felt, even at the lightest of touches. "Sorry," she said.

He turned to face her.

He looked at her.

Looked into her.

Then he put his arms around her.

This time it wasn't about sex. It was about comfort. And at that moment, he needed her more than she needed him.

After a moment he swallowed. She felt it, the shift in the dynamic. He got up and locked the door, leaving the key in the lock.

Leaving the key in the lock meant no one else could open the door.

She helped him out of his jacket, laying it on the floor next to the mattress beside her.

He made no attempt to undress her. There was no hurried fumble, no desperate hungry pawing in search of satisfaction. He just lay down on the mattress and held onto her as though they were the last moments of his life.

He sobbed until he finally fell asleep.

THIRTEEN

Konstantin slipped out through a cramped window in the back of the brothel.

The whore had been more than happy to play along with his game; it wasn't often that she was paid quite so well to spend a few hours in bed, on her own, with no one watching.

She agreed to lock the door and leave the window open for his return.

Better yet, she'd asked no questions, just taken half of the money he'd promised up front on the understanding that she would get the rest when he came back. Double if he was more than a couple of hours.

Of course, he wasn't an idiot. Greed meant that he had two hours. Any longer and she'd open her door for another client.

It was unlikely that the smoker would venture inside looking for him, but not impossible. More likely, though, he'd wait patiently until Konstantin finally emerged with a very self-satisfied smirk on his face. Of course, it'd be a different kind of satisfaction to the usual punter, but the smoker wouldn't know any better.

The taxi picked him up a couple of streets away.

He was well on the way to the airport before the prostitute settled back into her bed.

He'd seen a paperback on the bedside table—the same one he'd slammed at his hotel room wall. He'd refrained from saying anything about it. He doubted she was a literary critic, and he didn't have time for small talk.

Maybe he'd buy her a good book on his way back if he had time?

"That was quick, my Yankee friend," the driver said as Konstantin slipped into the back seat of the cab.

They'd agreed a meeting place before he'd gone inside the brothel, but he was sure that the driver had expected him to be a little longer than the fifteen minutes it had taken him to come to an arrangement with the girl and to walk to their rendezvous point. There hadn't been long enough to arrange for another cab, but the driver hadn't tripped any of the warning signals Konstantin looked for, so he had no reason to think he was anything other than he seemed to be. If the driver told anyone about his ruse later, it wouldn't matter. They'd be long gone, the op completed.

Konstantin smiled. "It'd been a while, if you catch my drift," he said, letting the driver think this particular American had no staying power.

"So, where to? Want to see if you can get drunk just as quickly?"

Konstantin found himself liking the guy.

Usually, he wanted taxi drivers to keep their mouths shut and drive. He wasn't interested in their wives, the state of the economy, the corrupt politicians or the latest celebrity scoop. But this guy had a little more about him. Konstantin needed to be a good judge of people. It kept him alive. He looked at the man in the rear-view mirror. Smiled. He could relax a little.

"Airport, please."

The taxi pulled back into traffic. The driver lapsed into silence as he concentrated on weaving in and out of lanes, leaning on his horn and mocking other drivers every now and then with some quick-fire repartee.

"So that was that your farewell to Israel?" The driver laughed. The man's laugh was infectious.

"No, I'm meeting someone."

"Ah, well, you want me to wait again? You can call me James. I'll be your personal driver; maybe you bring me a hat from gift shop? Make it look official?"

Konstantin laughed again. "That would be great, thanks."

"No problem, my friend. I'll be right here," he said as he pulled into a parking bay a few minute's walk from the terminal doors. It was a good spot. Airport security wouldn't try to move him on every five minutes.

Konstantin stepped out of the car, slammed his door, and then reached inside the driver's window. He pressed another couple of notes into the man's hand. He only glanced back once as he headed towards the terminal. The taxi driver was already settling back with his newspaper.

"How long have I got?" he asked, pressing a finger to his ear.

Lethe responded almost immediately: "The plane has just touched down. He's not carrying any luggage, so top end, he should be out within twenty minutes."

"Nice work."

"Nothing better to do, obviously."

There were times when Konstantin struggled to catch the nuances of Lethe's speech, and there were other times when they came through crystal-clear and dripping with sarcasm. He knew how hard the guy worked. Even though he did not have to take the risks that the rest of them did, he was in many ways the most dangerous of them all.

Konstantin took the chance to grab an overpriced bottle of water from one of the concessions while he waited.

He scanned the hall.

There was the chance someone would come to meet Nasri, but it seemed unlikely. Still, it didn't hurt to keep an eye on the clutch of people gathered around the arrivals gate. Maybe they'd be stupid enough to have a cardboard sign with Nasri's name written on it.

Or an eye patch...

The man seemed familiar.

Konstantin couldn't put a name to the face.

It took him a moment, and then he realized where he had seen him before. He fished out his mobile phone to check the photo of Saddiq.

Sure enough, there was Eye Patch, standing behind the man's left shoulder.

So he didn't need a sign at all.

He couldn't risk making verbal contact with Lethe.

It wasn't the illusion—that was easy enough to keep up just by holding a phone to his ear. It was the words themselves. There was nothing to say that Eye Patch was here alone. Konstantin couldn't afford to be overheard.

But he wasn't sure he'd be able to hang around long enough to hand over to Frost.

Eye Patch was here to take Nasri straight to Saddiq.

That accelerated things.

He needed to get in contact with Orla, but he couldn't while she was dark. The best he could do was to leave a message with Lethe, and hope she touched base. Frost would have to look after himself.

With luck, his taxi diver was still waiting for him outside. With even more luck, he'd be ready to follow the pair wherever they went without asking questions. That was a lot of luck to ask for.

He saw Nasri.

The man looked like he was used to getting his own way. He strode through the crowd as though he expected them all to step aside. Maybe he thought he was a modern day Moses, parting the Red Sea?

A tourist slowed in front of him.

Nasri pushed him aside without a moment's hesitation.

Konstantin would have known this was his man even without the photograph Lethe had downloaded for him. The picture looked as though it had been taken from a passport. He didn't want to know how Lethe had obtained it.

Konstantin took another step back.

Eye Patch stepped forward to greet Nasri.

They spoke quickly, in Arabic, before walking away together like old friends. Nasri refused to hand over his hand luggage, brushing aside Eye Patch's efforts to play the good host. That was enough to convince Konstantin that the object they were looking for was inside. Nasri looked like the kind of man who took pleasure in making people perform menial tasks for him. It was all about the big swinging dick of authority and power. And Nasri was a big swinging dick.

Konstantin waited until the two men were heading towards the exit before he made his move.

Part of him wanted to snatch the bag and run.

He might have been able to get out of the airport, but there was no guarantee he wouldn't end up being gunned down in cold blood. That was the thing about airports since 9/11. They were infested with paranoia. So even if he'd got the artefact in his hands, with no escape plan, he was screwed. Hell, even if he'd made it outside there was no guarantee Saddiq didn't have a small army out there waiting.

Moving now would tip his hand. Failure would let the wrong people know they knew about the ring and the connection with Saddiq.

So no.

No big hero moments.

"They're leaving now," he said. "I'll attempt to follow, but I suspect they will head straight into Palestine. Tell Frost I couldn't wait."

He didn't wait for a response.

He reached the door, feeling the sudden difference between the air-conditioned atmosphere inside the building and the sweltering dry heat of the outside world.

He didn't step through.

He took a sudden step back, almost colliding with an elderly women struggling with her wheeled suitcase.

He held up his hands in apology as he sidestepped to avoid sending her and her case sprawling.

The old lady smiled at him without causing a fuss.

Thankfully, the two men did not look back.

Neither did their driver.

He wasn't surprised to see that it was the same car that had been driving the cigarette smoker around.

Under-resourced, no doubt. His chain-smoking friend was still outside the brothel in the sweltering heat, so his car had been diverted for another job: picking up the merchandise.

The car started to move away, sliding into a queue of slow-moving traffic. Konstantin headed towards the taxi, only to see that it was already heading in his way.

"I saw you come out," the driver said as he clambered in. "What happened to your friend?"

"Friend?"

"You know, the man you'd come to meet?"

"Ah, right, yes. He's in the car three ahead of us. I need you to follow him."

"Follow him? Are you some kind of spy, my Yankee friend? Follow that cab! Is that what this is all about? I like it."

"Not exactly, no," Konstantin chuckled, making light of it. "It's just business. Turns out my friend is travelling with a rival. I want to know where he's going and what he's being offered, so I can make him a better offer."

"An offer he can't refuse? Works for me, Yankee Spy. The meter is running, and money is money." It was clear that the man was enjoying himself, as if this kind of thing happened to him every day. Maybe it did? Maybe the life of a taxi driver would make a great Hollywood movie? "You want me to keep a car in between us, like they do in the movies? So they don't know that they are being followed."

"Knock yourself out," Konstantin said. "Live the dream."

FOURTEEN

"Looks like it's just us," Lethe said. "Frost didn't make the rendezvous in time to make the pick-up. Konstantin had to split. If he's right, the Seal's heading your way. I've got a shot of the car and the driver and I'm sending that to you now."

Orla heard the ping that heralded the arrival of the email, but there was no point in looking at it now. She had to get herself mobile. The chances of there being any kind of car-hire service were less than zero. She could only mingle with the tourists for so long. Once they left the beaten track, she'd stick out like a sore thumb. Which left her with the options of buy, beg, borrow, or steal a car. The last option represented the most risk. It wasn't worth the risk. She'd have to try to buy something to get her around, or hire a local boy looking to make a few bucks for the morning playing chauffeur.

She remembered the Boy and how he had tried to teach her a little of his language, not realising that she was fluent. They had spent hours in the dark together in those last couple of days. He had done nothing more than hold her, talk, and sleep. It was those moments that made her feel worst about the way she'd used him to escape that place. There was always going to be a price to be paid, though; she knew that. He'd paid it. Sometimes it was difficult to detach from her emotions, and remember that it had been him or her. There was no saving them both.

Orla walked through the empty streets. A few dogs wandered along the sides of buildings. She couldn't afford to hang around for too long. The longer she was out here, the greater the chance of Nasri's car coming through. Lethe would do his best to keep track of the vehicle, but in the places like this, where there was an almost complete absence of CCTV and surveillance, and narrow streets made the consistency of satellite images difficult, the chances were that he'd lose it for stretches of time.

The first few cars she saw looked more like they'd been abandoned rather than parked. She doubted any of them would get her very far. If she wanted to get mobile, none of them would fit the bill.

She was about to give up and try to retrace her steps when she saw two teenagers polishing a moped that, like everything else on the street, had seen better days.

"Hi," she called to them, waving. One of them looked up, wanting to make a run for it but rooted to the spot. The other pushed out his chest and ran his fingers through his hair.

"Hey, babe," the second said. She realised he couldn't have been more than fifteen or sixteen, but he had the arrogant swagger of someone *much* older. "What can I do you for?"

If someone had used that tone on her in a bar, she'd have walked away. But she needed this arrogant little prick, so she bit her tongue. "This your bike, guys?"

"Sure is. You like it? I could take you for a ride."

I'm sure you *think* you could, she thought, and smiled. "What's not to like? It's a classic."

"My brother helped us," the younger boy said, obviously keen that they shouldn't take all the credit. It was an admirable quality life would stamp out of him soon enough.

"Yeah, but we found all the parts for him. He put it together. Teamwork."

Orla walked towards it and ran her hands across the rust-pitted chrome. If it worked, it would do the job. It wouldn't keep up if the car went at speed out on the open road, but on these narrow streets, it would be perfect. "How's she run?"

"Smooth," the boy said, grinning.

It might be, but he wasn't.

He threw one leg over the frame with an exaggerated flourish and kick-started the engine. It turned over on the first attempt. He twisted the throttle to show its power. It didn't exactly roar, but it didn't splutter, either. The noise was louder inside his own mind than it was in reality, but the engine sounded clean enough. It would do what she needed it to do. As long as it didn't fall apart in the process. The roads on this side of the border were in much worse repair than on the Israeli side, and they were bad enough.

"Is it for sale?"

"For sale?" He thought about it for a moment. "Maybe. I mean…if we can reach an agreement." He gave her a wink that made Orla's flesh crawl. She knew what was going through his mind. He'd just given her a glimpse of the man he was in danger of growing into. She'd be doing every woman in Palestine a favour if she broke his balls.

"No, it's not. My brother will kill us if we go and sell it now."

Orla smiled and turned her attention to the younger boy. "Well, how about we save your life? Can I hire it for a while?" He looked at her dubiously.

"What's to stop you just driving off with it?"

"I can give you a deposit." She pulled a billfold of American dollars from her back pocket. It was obviously more money than either of the boys had seen in their life. It was more than the moped was worth. She suspected that there was every chance that she would not see her money again and that she would end up abandoning the moped once she had finished with it. "I don't suppose I can get a receipt?" she asked, and the boys laughed.

Well, she wouldn't be getting that back on expenses.

The older boy looked a little disappointed as she drove away, even though he clutched the folded notes. The younger one was more interested in the money, or maybe he was just trying to work out how he was going to explain the moped's absence to his brother later on. She tooted once on the horn and waved, then she was gone around the corner.

Orla retraced her route.

"Have you been possessed by the spirit of Usain Bolt?" Jude said in her ear.

"He's not dead," Orla said.

"Well, okay, but that's just a technicality. You appear to be moving like greased lightning."

"I appropriated a rather battered moped."

"Nicely done that, woman. Okay, I've got eyes on the target. It's approaching the checkpoint now. Should be through on your side in a couple of minutes. You're going to need to get a shift on."

"I'm on it," she said, gunning the engine. The tyres sent stone chips spraying out in her wake.

FIFTEEN

Konstantin told the taxi driver to pull over before they reached the checkpoint.

There was no point taking unnecessary risks.

They were already more exposed than he would have liked.

His sole intention was to watch as the car went through. It was down to Lethe and Orla to pick it up on the other side.

There was one thing he could do...

He touched the St Christopher he wore beneath his shirt. It wasn't just a necklace, though the patron saint certainly looked after this particular traveller: it was a tracking device that broadcast a signal back to Nonesuch. If he took it off, he'd be flying blind. No, it was worse than that, it was more akin to jumping out of a plane without a parachute. His fist closed around the chain. Better to be without it here, than on the other side.

He broke the chain and pulled the pendant free. It amazed him that something so small was capable of doing so much.

"Okay, my friend; be ready to drive like a madman. We may need to make a quick getaway," Konstantin said, giving the driver a reassuring pat on the shoulder as he slid out of the car.

"I'll keep the engine running," the Israeli said, and then, almost as though it hadn't occurred to him until that very second, "You're not going to shoot anyone, are you?"

Konstantin smiled back at him.

It was a dangerous grin.

It said, you know…I just might.

And then he shook his head.

He had no intention of shooting anyone.

He needed to stay out of sight, but get close enough to plant the tracker. He skirted around the back of the cab, then sprinted through the dead man's land between the two cars, keeping low, running hard, then dropped below the line-of-sight out of the rear window. Breathing hard, he hunkered down and waited for his opportunity. The guard checking their documents ought to give him just the kind of distraction he needed, not that it would be a proper check. He'd have a few seconds, at best.

He turned slightly so he faced back the way he had come; it kept his face away from the men in the car.

In a single movement, he reached into the wheel-arch and allowed the magnetic back of the St Christopher to attach itself to the bodywork. It thunked into place.

He snatched his hand away as the car started to move again.

Konstantin remained where he was, letting the next car in the line pass him before he stood upright. He walked back to the taxi.

"Do we need to burn some rubber?"

Konstantin shook his head. "Not today. I've still got some time on the clock before we need to be back at the brothel, so drop me around the back again then drive around to the front and wait for me. It shouldn't take me long to finish my business."

The taxi driver laughed again. "You are a machine!"

*   *   *

The girl was fast asleep when he climbed in through her window.

The open book lay face down on her breasts, a pair of glasses perched at an angle on her face.

It wasn't her most seductive pose.

And it wouldn't have been good for business—smart women turned men off when they were paying for sex. They wanted the whore, not the Madonna. She looked so peaceful; he didn't want to wake her. She had kept her side of the bargain. He appreciated that. He left two hundred dollars—fifty more than they'd agreed—on the cabinet beside her bed, and let himself silently out of the room.

At the front door he slipped the madam another note to make sure that the girl remained undisturbed.

The taxi was waiting outside, ready for him.

Konstantin paused for a moment, breathing deeply and stretching, like a man who'd just spent the afternoon fucking and was savouring the vitality that came with it. He gave the cigarette smoking man a glance. He was talking rapidly into a mobile phone—calling in for transport, no doubt—but his driver was too far away to get back in time to tail the Russian. Konstantin felt a little sorry for the guy. There was nothing worse than struggling to do a job without the resources that were needed, especially when going up against a better man. And Konstantin was in no doubt that he was the better man. If the smoker thought he'd been inside the brothel all this time, then there was no point in making the man suffer. He wasn't needlessly cruel. That wasn't his style. He crossed the road and walked towards the man. The smoker turned and started to walk away. He wasn't exactly blending in to the background.

"Excuse me," Konstantin called. "Can I bum a light off you?"

The man stopped. He turned. Hesitated. Then started to walk back towards the Russian. Konstantin could see the mixed emotions playing across the man's face as he tried to work out if his cover had been blown. In his place, Konstantin would have just kept on walking.

The man offered the glowing tip of his own cigarette, but Konstantin had no need for it. "Thanks," he said, offering a shrug. "But no thanks. I've changed my mind." The man looked confused. Konstantin decided to help him out. "I just thought I'd let you know I'm heading back to my hotel now. I can give you a lift, if you like? No? Okay, well, there should be a bus before too long. I'll only be at the hotel for as long as it takes to sort out a flight home, so in case I don't see you again, give yourself a pat on the back. Job well done. You might as well finish early."

He walked back towards the taxi.

All things being equal, Orla would already be on the target's tail.

There was nothing else he could do now.

He'd be out of the country in a matter of hours, and heading back to a cooler climate, which suited him just fine.

SIXTEEN

Orla picked up the car without any problems.

It was less than a mile from the border crossing.

She hung back as far as she dared. The traffic thinned. She couldn't always manage to keep a car or two between them. She weaved in and out of their line of sight, feeling every stone and pothole beneath her wheels.

The car slowed slightly, and the gap between them closed.

It turned right without indicating.

Had they made her?

No.

No, they were still oblivious.

As the car turned, she caught a glimpse of one of the men in the back seat: the Beast, in his eye patch.

She felt a surge of fear. It verged on panic and threatened to overwhelm her. She gripped the throttle tighter. She breathed hard. Fast. She felt herself going light-headed as she struggled to master her fear.

There was no question about it: it was him.

She wasn't sure where they were, but it felt as though they were heading back towards the debris-strewn streets where she'd obtained the moped. That wasn't good. If the kids made a fuss and she was seen, then there was no telling what might happen. She didn't want the boys getting caught up in crossfire. The thought brought her to the here and now. To the reality of the present.

She was getting careless.

She'd allowed her mind to lose its focus.

She battered down the memories of those dark days of Jenin, before they could cripple her.

They drove on.

As the buildings became fewer and fewer, her presence was going to become more noticeable.

"Okay, hot stuff, got you both on the big screen. Smile." Lethe's voice came through the earpiece. "You can drop back if you need to. Koni's tracker's in place. There's no escape now."

Lethe wasn't a field operative. He'd never worked outside of Nonesuch, but that didn't mean he didn't have a good understanding of what being on the ground meant, or what was needed. It didn't hurt that technology had caught up with their needs.

Orla eased off the throttle and allowed the gap between her and the car to widen until she was watching the cloud of dust behind it.

Even though the technology meant she didn't need to maintain visual contact at all times, she was reluctant to let the car completely out of her sight. Every now and then, the old ways were the best. And technology could always fail—and that applied every bit as much to the moped rattling beneath her as it did to the hi-tech tracking device that Konstantin had fixed to the car.

After a couple of miles, the car turned left, leaving the main road in favour of a very dusty track between buildings that seemed to lead nowhere.

She rode straight past the turning. She couldn't stop to look: that would raise suspicion. So, after another half-mile she pulled over to the side of the road and waited for Lethe's update.

She didn't have to wait long.

"The track goes about a mile and a half and dead-ends at a cluster of buildings. They look like farmhouses. Maybe a kibbutz? Five vehicles, including the car you've been following. I can make out maybe a dozen people milling around. That's just on the outside. There's no way of knowing how many are inside."

Orla felt a strange weakness steal through her legs. The moped was all that stopped them from buckling. She tightened her grip and fought against bile rising in her throat. Memories came rushing to the surface, and no matter how hard she tried, she couldn't push them back down.

"Orla?"

She spat onto the dusty ground. The foul taste remained in her mouth. She knew that it wouldn't wash away. It wasn't that kind of taste.

"Orla? You okay?" Lethe's voice was insistent. Concerned.

"Still here," she said.

"Looks like there's some kind of generator behind the main block. There's certainly some heat coming off it."

"Okay. I'm going to hang back until it starts to get dark. Then I'll go in." She breathed deeply. It wasn't a farmhouse. It wasn't a kibbutz. It was all that was left of the refugee camp. She'd followed them to Jenin. She was back on the threshold of Hell. There were no gods, but there was one, very real, devil. The Beast. "Let me know if it looks like anyone is leaving."

It couldn't be the same place.

It couldn't be.

It couldn't.

But it was.

SEVENTEEN

The last time she was here:

The door burst open.

The unmistakeable shape of the Beast stood in the doorway.

He barked an order.

The Boy struggled to his feet, grabbing the clothes he had discarded.

He stood between the doorway and Orla, pulling his trousers up.

Orla dressed quickly. Silently. She knew that the Boy would feel the Beast's anger first. She made sure that she didn't make eye contact. She knew how dangerous he was. She didn't need to challenge him. Not now. This had to be about her money. That meant it could be her only chance. She was ready.

The Beast pushed the Boy to the ground as he fumbled with his belt. He went sprawling.

"She goes now!"

"Have they agreed to pay?" the Boy asked, he didn't try to stand.

"Of course they haven't," Orla said. She wanted to goad an emotional response out of the men. She needed them to be at each other's throats, just for a second. One flash of anger. That would give her a chance. "And now you've run out of patience. The best thing you can do is get it over with. Tell him the truth. You've come to kill me."

"No, no, that can't be right. They'll pay eventually," the Boy said, hopefully, stupidly. "They have to."

"No they don't," Orla said. "We don't trade with terrorists or kidnappers."

"You knew?"

"I knew."

"Good," the Beast said, and raised his sub-machine gun. He motioned for her to move, prodding her towards the door with the barrel. He backed around the room. Orla moved slowly, not taking her eyes off him. She wasn't about to risk any sudden moves. The Beast was jumpy. Anything—any sound, any wrong move—could have him pulling the trigger. Every heartbeat was precious. Insects, birds, even hummingbirds, and humans all shared the same basic amount of heartbeats over the course of their lifetimes. Some burned through them much faster than others. Orla slowed her breathing. She refused to panic. Inhale. Exhale. Inhale. It was the pattern of life. It was survival.

The Boy grabbed at the Beast's leg. He shrieked. It was barely recognisable as a human sound; it was so full of desperation, hopelessness and fury. The Beast swung the butt of the gun down hard, connecting with the Boy's jaw with a sickening thud. The impact drove him back down, leaving him in a whorish sprawl on the floor.

This was going to get out of control fast.

Orla grabbed her jacket. Let them think she was lying to herself, let them think she thought she had a chance, when the only chance was that she'd be dead in a few minutes. She knew what they'd do: they'd march her away from the buildings, somewhere more remote. Somewhere her corpse wouldn't stink up their encampment. And then they'd shoot her. In the face. It was personal, now. The Beast would want to disfigure her, leave nothing recognisable should her body ever be found. They'd smash her jaw and drive the hilt of the rifle into her teeth again and again until dental records would be useless. They'd cut her hands off, or burn them. No fingerprints. After that, maybe she'd be buried; more likely she wouldn't. They'd expect the scavengers to pick away at her bones and clean up their mess. It wouldn't matter to her. She'd be a long time gone by then.

The Boy groaned on the floor.

It didn't sound good.

For a moment, she thought she might have lost her only ally.

Orla shuffled slowly towards the doorway.

She needed the time for her eyes to adjust to the daylight.

Even so, it wouldn't help much; she'd been locked away in the dark for too long. Even the slightest hint of sunlight burned. Her eyes streamed with tears before she was out of the door. She fought to stay calm. Panic would kill her. She was almost outside though when Boy lashed out again, clawing at the Beast's ankles.

The Beast swung around, flailing out with the butt of the gun.

The Boy held on long enough.

With the Beast's back turned to her, Orla struck. She reached around the Beast's neck quickly, yanking his head back, and drove the pin of the Greenpeace badge she'd clutched in her clenched fist deep into the Beasts eye.

He howled in pain.

His hand came up, clutching at her hand even as she twisted the badge, working the needle-point though his eye, piercing the cornea and the lens, leaking the vitreous liquid out over her fingers.

His trigger finger tightened, releasing a burst of bullets.

The Boy was dead before the cry had even reached his lips.

There was no time for sentiment. The Boy had given her a chance of life. She intended to take it.

The Beast half-staggered, twisting in her arms.

Orla let him.

As he turned, she drove her knee into the Beast's balls, and tore the gun from his grasp in one brutally efficient movement.

He doubled up, incoherent words burbling off his lips. There was blood on his face. He'd pissed himself. She could smell it. She didn't care. There was never any dignity in death. She drove her elbow into the side of his head. The Beast's legs buckled. He fell.

She didn't waste time checking on the Boy. He was dead. The hole in the middle of his face was unmistakable.

She put the muzzle up against his face, forcing it between his teeth until he gagged on the cold metal.

She stared at him until he opened his eyes and looked at her.

There was fear in his eyes.

"Now you know what I've been living with," she said. There was no emotion in the words. "But I am kinder than you."

She squeezed the trigger.

It clicked dryly.

Empty.

She cast the gun aside. "Seems like god looks after bastards," she said coldly.

The Beast started to laugh.

She kicked him in the side of the face, hard, caving in part of his skull.

She left him for dead.

Outside, she heard voices.

They weren't raised. There was no urgency to them.

She realised that they'd just assumed the Beast had decided to kill her inside the prison, rather than take her off towards the forest.

She could live with that.

Literally.

Orla peered through the narrow crack created by the hinge of the open door. Two men approached her cell. Neither of them appeared to be in any great hurry. Good. One of them carried a submachine gun loosely at his side; the other had a Jericho 941 in the holster at his hip. He walked with a swagger, like a cowboy new in town.

She had no idea of how many she was up against, but it was more than two, and her only chance of getting out of there came down to just how much of a surprise she could spring. Without a gun of her own, she needed a miracle.

She couldn't deal with the Beast twice.

She'd rather die.

And this was her opportunity to put that to the test.

She leaned against the wall, just inside the doorway, watching the shadows.

They stepped into the doorway, and hesitated fatally, not understanding what they saw. Orla didn't hesitate. She lashed out with her left arm, driving her elbow into the lead man's face. His nose ruptured beneath the impact. He dropped the sub-machine gun. She grabbed it, and rolled, and came up firing.

The two men dropped without a single shot fired in retaliation.

She just had to put as much distance between her and this place as she could.

Wherever 'this place' was.

She'd been blindfolded as soon as they'd taken her, and then thrown in the back of a windowless van. She remembered the van. It was burned into her memory, or rather, the stench of it was. Dead animals. At first she'd thought they'd used it to move bodies, but later she'd caught a glimpse of it being used to bring food into the camp.

She stepped out into the full glare of sunlight.

It was blinding.

Truly.

She couldn't see, but she couldn't wait.

She didn't have a choice.

She ran blindly, trusting instinct and willing her vision to clear.

There were blurred, dark shapes in front of her. Cars. Four of them. One was bigger, bulkier than the others: the van. There were advantages to it, she knew. It was reliable. Used regularly. But it wasn't built for off-road, and that was the clincher. She moved on to the next blurred shape, her vision focussing a little more with each step: an old, battered Land Rover. That was a more appealing prospect. Its wheels were built for rough terrain.

She ran for it.

More voices behind her.

Too many footsteps, running hard.

It was now or never.

She made a run for the Land Rover. She tried to keep the other vehicles between her and her kidnappers. Her first instinct was to shoot out the tyres of the van as she passed it, but that would have told them exactly where she was. She couldn't risk it.

They didn't know where she was.

She saw one of them duck into the small, squat building she had been held in. She kept her head down, running hard. From the outside, the prison block seemed larger, built with concrete blocks.

If she'd had the time she would have brought the whole place to the ground, but she'd have to leave that to the IDF's tanks. They'd flatten the place the moment she could get confirmation to them that their targets were inside.

She didn't look back.

She'd rather die than spend another minute in the compound, not knowing when the door would swing open again. Not knowing when the Beast would come back to inflict his 'passion' on her.

Raised voices.

They'd found the bodies.

The relief at finding the keys in the ignition of the Land Rover was palpable. Her heartbeat raced, burning through more of its lifetime's worth of beats.

She climbed into the driver's side and slid behind the wheel.

She put the gun in her lap, leaving both of her hands free.

She turned the key. The engine turned over. She turned the key again. It caught, but didn't exactly roar into life.

But it was noise. It was out of place. And that meant the men would come running. She forced the car into gear and swung around. The air was shredded by gunfire. Bullets whistled over and under the Land Rover. One shattered the rear window, leaving an opaque spider-web where there had been a view of the prison building. She didn't waste time trying to return fire. It was all about distance now. Movement. She floored the accelerator, and kept her foot pressed down hard, wrestling with the wheel.

Bullets struck the bodywork, sending up a shower of sparks and shards of metal like shrapnel.

The windscreen shattered.

Orla felt a sliver of glass embed itself in her cheek.

It stung, but there was no real pain. The receptors of her brain were drowning in pure adrenalin.

The Land Rover juddered and shuddered along the rocky ground, spitting stones and gravel in its wake as the engine whined. Orla desperately tried to keep the wheels on the rutted track, wrestling with the wheel.

She manipulated the pedals, changing up to a shriek from the gearbox.

The front wheel hit a pothole, causing the entire cab to lurch forward alarmingly, and the sub-machine gun to slide off her lap.

She didn't care.

She stared fixatedly forward.

Another staccato burst of gunfire raked the air, but it was further away now.

She had no idea how far the track ran. It wasn't a road. It was nothing more than hard-packed dirt sprinkled with shale. And it was so narrow the wheels were in danger of going off the road every time she hit a bump.

The engine whined. It wasn't built for this. She took the chance to shift through the gears again, changing her position. That move, as small as it was, meant her head was more exposed.

It was greeted by another rattle of gunfire.

She could have sworn she felt a bullet graze her cheek.

She didn't flinch.

In the rear-view mirror, she could see the cloud of dust being thrown up by her own wheels, and through it, in the distance, the van following her. It was too far behind for her to try and shoot, and for them to shoot at her. She kept her foot pressed hard to the floor. The engine whined as it strained to reach the speed she demanded, but she was in control.

Finally, the rutted track met a well-used road.

She swung to the right, into the sun.

She wasn't sure what country she was in, never mind what road she was on or where she was heading. But if she was in Palestine, like she thought, she needed to get to the sea.

EIGHTEEN

No matter how hard she tried to convince herself that this wasn't the same place, that the IDF had flattened the entire compound when they'd bulldozed the refugee camp it serviced, there was no doubt that it was.

The Beast had brought her back to Hell.

She could have killed him when she had the chance.

It was a long time ago. Things changed. The memory was unreliable, at best. But they'd been the worst days of her life, and they were burned into her. So it didn't matter that she'd only caught a brief glance of the land around the compound as she'd driven out of there, or that she'd only seen the outside of the building for a minute as she ran, she knew it because it was ingrained on her soul.,It was Hell.

The van, fallen into decay, stood guard like Cerberus.

She'd ridden the moped as far as she had dared, then taken it off-road and hidden it out of sight in the undergrowth.

The hike in the ever-dimming light wasn't a comfortable one.

More than once she'd heard the hiss of a snake and the *whisper-rustle* of something moving softly in the sand.

She had settled herself into a deep crevice in the hillside, using the shadows to hide herself. She had a clear view of the encampment without being visible to a casual onlooker.

That was all well and good, but there were other creatures out there that would consider places like this to be their shelter from the blazing sun. They'd be venturing out now as the land began to cool. She could only hope she wasn't sleeping in one of their beds.

"You got anything for me yet?" she whispered, her finger on the ear bud.

"Six men," Lethe said. "Five of them in the long building, but the heat sources are scattered." So they weren't all in the same room, she thought, picturing the layout of the prison block mentally. "The other one's outside."

"Standing guard?"

"Taking a piss," he said.

Orla raised her binoculars.

She could see the man at the far side of the compound.

He had his back to her, but she was sure that he was zipping himself up.

Was he supposed to be a lookout, or had he just stepped outside to relieve himself?

Five men, that was all she had to concentrate on.

One of them was the man who had brought the ring here, meaning he wasn't a fighter, he was a broker. *If* their intelligence was correct.

What she still didn't really understand was, what she was doing there?

She was sure that the old man was keeping things from her.

She couldn't have said why. It was all gut-instinct. But there was something he wasn't saying.

"He's moving your way," Lethe's voice whispered in her ear.

She pressed herself further into her hiding place.

She needed to get into the compound, but there was no way that she was going to be able to do that safely while they had someone patrolling it.

She looked up at the sun. It was getting late. The chances were that no one would be leaving tonight.

Anyone trying to cross into Israel at night would raise far more suspicions than they would if they went with the daily tramp of workers in the morning or late afternoon.

That gave her some time at least.

She waited until the guard had done a circuit, keeping a track of the amount of time he took to complete it. He had done three turns of the perimeter by the time she was close enough to take care of him. She only moved when she was absolutely sure that she wouldn't be seen. She moved from hiding place to hiding place, choosing each one carefully along the way. Waiting wasn't going to be a problem. She had time. As long as she didn't screw up the kill. That was the key. If the guard managed to raise the alarm, she'd be in deep shit.

She needn't have worried.

The man lit a cigarette and perched himself on a boulder, savouring the smoke.

Orla seized the opportunity with both hands.

She closed the gap, moving silently. It took her seven seconds to reach him. He never knew she was there. She had the garrotte around his neck and had pulled it tight before he could gurgle. He grasped at the wire, pulling, trying to work his fingers under it even as it cut into his throat. He kicked out, heels scuffing against the dusty ground. She pulled tighter, choking the air off. She pushed her knee into the base of his spine and pulled tighter. Blood flowed down over her hands. She pulled tighter, the wire slicing into his windpipe. He gave up. His legs twitched once. Twice. Then he slumped against her, a deadweight. The garrotte was all that kept him upright.

Orla relaxed her grip.

She let the body fall to the ground, and then retrieved the wire.

She drew it across the dead man's jacket to wipe it clean.

There was still blood on her hands.

She ignored it.

"One down," she said.

Orla knew that Lethe was listening, but just this once, the words weren't for him.

She dragged the body out of sight, relieving the dead man of his gun. An IDF-issue Jericho.

She felt better for having it in her hand.

She felt alive.

This time, she would make sure she had one shot left for the Beast.

NINETEEN

It hadn't taken long to sort out the flight home, but Konstantin wasn't particularly enamoured with the idea of having to kick his heels until the following morning.

He could have left earlier, but that would have meant arriving a lot later at the other end. The train—and that was one thing this kind of climate wasn't good for, a long, air-conditioningless train journey—would have taken forever, so an extra night in the hotel and a few hours in an airport lounge to come didn't seem like such a hardship.

His phone rang. Lethe's name flashed up.

"Hope you've not packed your bags yet," Lethe said.

"I have no luggage," the Russian said, matter-of-factly. He shifted on the bed and held the phone away from his ear so Lethe could hear the complaining squeak of bedsprings. "But I do have luxury accommodation."

"Sounds like you've got company."

"Funny. You need something? Or is this a piss-the-Russian-off social call?"

"The old man wants to know if you would mind hanging around for another day or so, just in case."

"Just in case of what?"

"You know he worries."

"She's a big girl."

"That she is. But it's that place."

"You want me to go in and perform an exfiltration?"

"Not yet. But—"

"But if someone has to, I'm the man to do it."

"It's you or Frosty, or you and Frosty. It's just in case the shit hits the fan."

"And my flight?"

"I've already postponed it."

"So this is more of an order than a request?"

"You know the old man wouldn't explicitly order you to stick around, but I know he'd appreciate it."

"At least tell me there's something you want me to do rather than twiddle my thumbs."

"Just sit tight."

"Hurry up and wait."

"No need to hurry. Enjoy the bed for a while. Read a book."

"Funny guy. I know a taxi driver you'd get on well with." He hung up and slumped back on the bed. He stared reluctantly at the paperback still lying on the floor where he had thrown it.

"The glamorous life of a super hero," he said to no-one but the woodlice he shared the room with. He wondered if the chain-smoker was still waiting outside. Maybe he should go down and shoot the shit with him? Teach him some basic tradecraft?

It was only a few minutes later when his phone beeped. It was an incoming text message. One word: Ear bud.

"I'm here," he said, still pressing the phone into position.

When he had a job to do, he forgot that the thing was even in place, but whenever he was resting, it felt like the most uncomfortable thing in the world, so he took it out.

"Finally. Okay, that's everyone," Lethe said, before the old man's voice took over.

"There's been a development," Sir Charles said. Konstantin didn't like the way he said that. A development. That was never good. "I wanted to tell you all at the same time. Saves repeating myself. So let's keep it brief. Save your questions until after I have finished speaking. Understood?" There were murmurs of agreement as each of the team signalled their assent.

"Very good. Our latest intelligence suggests that the Israelis have identified the compound where the Seal is currently being examined. Mr Lethe's information was very helpful, including satellite imagery identifying how many people they had on site. The IDF have just informed me that they believe the people behind this have the capability of building a dirty bomb, using nuclear material they have obtained from Iraq."

No one said anything. "The usual response from an alert like this would be for the borders with Palestine to be completely sealed. No one in, no one out. Tanks would be rolling into the West Bank as we speak, and if they had pinpointed the presence of the material, they would already have missiles pointed at least in its approximate direction. Needless to say, Orla is in there. And under normal circumstances, she would be my primary concern; *but* they've not done any of these things."

"What do you mean?" It was Frost.

"I mean that instead of shutting up shop they've relaxed border controls as of midnight tonight."

"Why on earth would they want to do that?" Larkin asked.

"Shit," said Konstantin. He knew. There was only one answer that made sense to the Russian. "They want the bomb to go off."

"I believe you have hit the nail on the head, Konstantin. They *want* the bomb to go off, but more specifically than that, they want it to go off on Israeli soil. A dirty bomb detonating in Jerusalem. Think about it. It would be an atrocity. All bets would be off. The Israelis would be free to deal with the Palestinians as they saw fit, without fear of reprisals from the West."

"And if Iran decides to throw its weight behind the Palestinians," Frost said, "then it might just give the Americans the excuse they need to deal with Iran once and for all." He wasn't wrong.

"This has been bubbling away for a long time," the old man agreed. "Now that the borders are about to open, I don't think we've got a choice. Orla's at ground zero. She can't deal with this alone."

"You only have to say the word," said Konstantin.

"Consider this the word. While there's no *immediate* danger, I want you to remain on the Israeli side of the strip. The fact that you don't want the bomb to detonate makes you the only person any of us can trust."

"And the authorities? High profile targets? Anyone we need to babysit?"

"Strangely enough, both the Israeli Prime Minister and his deputy are out of the country at the moment—a hurriedly arranged diplomatic mission to Russia."

"Well out of harm's way." Lethe said.

"There is growing sympathy for the Jewish situation in Russia," Konstantin said. "Many of the oligarchs are from Jewish families. While they may not come out and join the fight on the side of the Israelis, they won't speak out against them. If aid was sought in the form of weaponry, that would be different. It's in their interests to promote chaos in the Middle East."

"We have to stop it," Orla cut him off.

They fell silent.

Konstantin hadn't even realised she was on the line. She was the one on the ground. She had command of the op. It was as simple as that. She was eyes-on.

"How are things looking?" Frost asked.

"One dead guard, five men inside the main compound. The deal's not going down yet, though. I think they're waiting for someone else. Sooner or later, though, someone's going to come looking for their dead friend. When they can't find him, I may have to make a move."

"I believe there are a number of vehicles in the compound?" the old man said.

"Excluding the car I followed over the border, there are a couple of old Ladas. They've seen better days. And there's a van. They were both here last time," she sniffed. Konstantin caught it. Just the slightest hesitation. "And a new Land Rover."

"The last time?" asked Konstantin, knowing what those three words meant.

There was silence on the line.

"This is where I was held."

There was nothing he could say to that. Nothing any of them could.

It was an open secret that she'd been captured in an op that had gone south. What that entailed: well, none of them talked about it, but Konstantin could guess.

But going back there.

To the compound.

He shook his head.

This was bad. She wouldn't be detached. She'd got an emotional connection with the place. Triggers. She was at risk. It didn't matter how good she was at her job: this was bad. He clenched his fist.

"You should have told me," he said.

"And what difference would it have made?"

"You're invested," Konstantin said. "You're putting yourself at risk."

"There's no one who knows this place better than I do," she objected.

"You shouldn't be there alone."

"But I am," she said.

"Orla, dear girl, one question: are you able to carry out the task at hand?" Sir Charles asked.

"Of course I am," she said without missing a beat.

Konstantin knew this game. He knew the old man too well. He'd put her in an impossible position. She couldn't give any other answer. More than that, she'd given it publicly. The old man's hands were going to be clean no matter what happened. It was easy to believe Sir Charles Wyndham was one of them, just like Lethe, but he wasn't. He wasn't the kindly father figure. He was a political animal. He had his own agenda. He was like a chess player making his gambits, pushing them around the board. But did that mean he was really capable of making a pawn sacrifice? Or were they more than that? Was Orla his queen? Ronan Frost his king? Konstantin and Noah his knights?

"I would ask for one thing," Orla said.

"Ask."

"Ronan, look, this isn't ideal; but if I they get the bomb out…"

"You'd like me to stick around as a failsafe?"

"Precisely."

This wasn't a show of weakness or a cry for help; this was purely practicality. Orla was a pro. They were a team. The stakes had just been ramped up, but the cards in their hand had remained the same.

"Check the Land Rover out. It's the most reliable of the vehicles."

"What are you thinking?"

"Belfast," Frost said.

"A car bomb," Konstantin agreed. It made sense. It was the easiest way to transport a dirty bomb over the border, even if the normal border checks were being applied.

"Makes sense," Orla agreed.

"Can you get close enough to switch the tracking device?" Lethe asked.

"Where is it?"

"Rear wheel arch, passenger side," Konstantin told her.

"Sure."

"Good. Do it," said the old man. "Orla, you'll need to follow the Seal. Frost, we can't risk that bomb going off."

"Understood." Frost said.

"Do you think they're connected?" Larkin asked. "Seems unlikely they're pure coincidence."Larkin asked.

"The same people are involved," the old man said. "So they're connected. We'll worry about how once we've stopped the damn thing going off."

"I've got some more material on the ring if anyone's interested?" said Lethe.

"Not for me," said Orla. "There's movement here."

The *click* of her disconnection was barely audible, but it was a moment of change. They all knew that she was walking into the lion's den. There was nothing that any of them could do. She was on her own. And she'd decided to make it that way.

TWENTY

Orla's heart raced.

A man emerged from the building.

Not a man.

A monster.

A beast.

Despite the passage of time, the distance and the poor light, there was no doubt about who it was.

He had haunted her nightmares for so long now. Every movement, every line in his face, all of it, was ingrained on her memory.

She raised the sub-machine gun she'd taken from the dead guard.

She trained it on him. There were no crosshairs. No sights to hold him in, making him a dead man. She didn't need them. When the time came, she wouldn't miss. But for now, the distance between them was too great for her to risk squeezing a burst off. She changed the setting to single shot.

He lit a cigarette. The sudden glow from the tip lit his face, casting half of it in darker shadow. She saw the eye patch.

She wanted to pull the trigger.

She wanted to punch a hole through his skull and spray blood and brains against the wall behind him. She would have enjoyed the look of surprise on his face as he tried to understand that he'd just died. Smoking kills, she thought. She didn't take the shot, but only because she knew the elevation, the distance, the wind, the bad light, all of them combined made it a difficult shot, and she wanted to know he was dead the minute she pulled the trigger. No second chances. She wanted him to see her face. And she wanted him to die slowly.

The Beast didn't look for the missing guard. He walked across to the Land Rover. Frost was on the money. The car was important to him. He only circled it, resting his hand on the metalwork at one point like a proud parent. She realised what was missing: floodlights. There was no exterior lighting anywhere in the compound. It made sense: lights increased the risk of drawing prying eyes. It also helped her, so she wasn't complaining.

He stubbed out his cigarette on the wall, and then flicked it away.

He waited outside a moment longer, lost in thought, then went back inside and closed the door behind him.

Orla broke cover.

She skirted the edge of the compound, moving fast but making sure she kept her speed steady. It was the erratic nature of movement that drew the eye, not movement itself. She made herself small and made sure the moon wasn't at her back. That was the best she could do. There was cover, but it was sparse. It was a gamble, but it was unlikely anyone else would come outside for a while. Anyone who'd wanted a smoke break would have followed the Beast outside. She could have asked Lethe, but she didn't know what kind of surveillance tech they had in there—maybe they were monitoring the airwaves like he was? Always assume the enemy is at least as smart as you are, and twice as good at their job. That's what the old man said. It was a mantra to live by.

Primary Objective: make sure Frost could complete the mission if she fucked up.

Secondary Objective: don't fuck up.

Because of the darkness, it took her longer to locate the St. Christopher hidden in the wheel arch than it should have. She was shaking, she realised.

It didn't help that they'd parked ready to drive out, meaning the tracker was on the side closest to the main block of the buildings.

Against the wall of the cell she'd nearly died in.

She couldn't think about it: the filthy mattress where she'd been raped by the Boy and the Beast and anyone else they thought would enjoy trying to break her. That was men: they imagined that rape was the worst possible violation for a woman. They imagined numbness and hate and self-loathing; they didn't ever imagine survival or strength. They didn't understand. She had won, that day. They hadn't broken her. She'd been tempered, like a sword.

She ducked beneath the line of the car as movement cast a shadow in the window above.

No one else stepped outside.

She fumbled around the rough metal, running her hand over every inch of it until she found the medallion and prised it free.

Staying low, Orla scurried around the side of the car, keeping it between her and the building, and then sprinted across the open courtyard to the Land Rover.

She dropped to the ground, dead still, listening.

Nothing.

She didn't move.

Still nothing.

And still she didn't move.

She listened to the sounds of the night: the ticking of the compound's tin roof as it cooled, the rustle of the breeze through the bare trees in the distance, the forlorn sound of a car far, far away in the night, driving somewhere safe.

She rose to a crouch, and then set the St. Christopher inside the Land Rover's wheel arch, making sure it was secure.

She wasn't sure what she was looking for exactly. The explosive mechanism and the depleted Uranium didn't have to be combined; a single explosion would be enough to blow the container open and release its lethal material into the air. There wouldn't be a warning sign or a 'danger explosives' sticker. It could have been a holdall on the backseat, it could have been inside the seats themselves or wired to the engine block or the axle or... It didn't matter what the bomb looked like. It was all about the effect. All about panic. Twisted metal, crushed concrete and cinder blocks and blood. It was all about destruction.

And thinking logically, if the two elements *could* be kept separate, then the chance of neutralising the bomb either doubled or halved.

She was thinking in terms of escalation: the Americans would wade into the conflict in the event of successful detonation. These were nuclear contaminants. It was the kind of strike Homeland Security dreaded. The explosion didn't have to be huge for the effect to be devastating. But without the Uranium, it was a car bomb, and denouncing a cowardly act of terrorism was about as hands on as the US could get.

From the Palestinians' perspective, keeping the two component parts apart until the moment of detonation made sense, too. It was safer, harder to detect and easier to move.

The question was whether or not she could identify the vehicle carrying the depleted Uranium before the Beast crossed over into Israel. It didn't matter what their target was. It could be the Dome on the Rock, for all it mattered. And thinking about that, she suddenly thought about Solomon, the Seal, and the site of the first Temple, and wondered if that wasn't the plan. Detonate the dirty bomb on one of the most holy shrines in the world, not just to Christians, but also to Muslims and Jews alike. It was a sucker-punch. But no. Not if they wanted the Iranians to come in: they couldn't detonate it on the site where Mohammed ascended. The Wailing Wall made a more logical target.

It was what she would have done—and if she followed the old man's logic that meant it was what the Beast was doing.

But would the Israelis welcome that kind of strike?

Dear God...

There was movement again.

This time someone opened the door.

A billow of smoke escaped into the night air.

Orla was fairly sure it was the driver.

He was overweight—not a lot, but enough for her to notice. Probably not military. Weight issues usually meant a lack of discipline. Military men were regimented, focused in the extreme. Disciplined, in other words. Causes, however, attracted all kinds of people.

She crouched behind the Land Rover, holding her breath. She willed the man to stay where he was. If he didn't, she'd have to kill him. It'd be like playing Ten Little Indians. Eventually, someone would notice their numbers were down. And then they'd come looking.

She rested a hand on the spare wheel to support herself.

Her fingers traced the deep tread of the unused tyre, complete with the tiny fragments of rubber that would rub away within moments of being used.

Two minutes later the driver was back inside.

Orla examined the spare wheel a little closer.

New. Very new. But not only the tyre: the entire wheel. Newer than the Land Rover. That one little detail rang alarm bells. Her hand was resting no more than an inch from the explosives, the nuclear material, or both.

She weighed up the risks and triggered the ear bud anyway. She whispered, "Lethe? You hear me?"

"Your wish is my command," came the reply. "I never understood that. Your wish is my command...anyway, go for it."

"I think the Land Rover's hot," she said. "Don't know if it is the Uranium, the explosives or both, but I think it's loaded. So if the boss just wants me to put a stop to this, the obvious thing to do is steal it. Frost can take a look at it when it's a long way away from here."

"Okay. Makes sense. But what are the chances of you being able to do that without anyone noticing?"

"Drive away with their bomb in the middle of the night? I'd say pretty bloody slim. It's dead here. I mean, silent. They can probably hear me in the hills ten miles away. But, maybe if everyone is asleep, I could try and roll it down the road a bit before I fire it up. Even then, it'll probably wake someone up. Let the old man decide." She broke the connection and returned her attention to the spare wheel.

The night sky was clear.

She had enough light to see by, thanks to the full moon.

She tried to reason it out: if the wheel contained nuclear material, it would be easy to transport it without raising suspicion. Maybe the rubber was part of some sort of shielding? The tyre could easily be lined with something else. And the Uranium was stable. They could drive around with it in place without risk of it going off. Explosives were different. You couldn't risk driving them over terrain like this with the detonator in place. C4, easy to pack into the hollowed-out tyre, wouldn't go off without a detonator. Keep the two separate, and it was safe as houses. Jam the detonator into the rubber, and it was a different story.

Thinking didn't help.

Lethe came back to her: "The old man says don't risk compromising yourself. Your safety is paramount. That was it. The full extent of his wisdom. I'd say he was pretty pissed off that you didn't let him know this was the same place you were held."

"It's my problem. I'll deal with it."

"I'm sure you will. So's he."

All the details of Jenin, the Beast, the Boy and what she'd gone through, were in her debrief. She hadn't held anything back. There was no way she could have gotten away with lying. They were also in her psych-profile. 18 months in therapy was a lot of confession time. A lot of laying the soul bare. A lot of truth. She didn't have any secrets from the old man. He knew it all, even if the others didn't.

They all had their personal tragedies though; even the old man.

Lethe was the exception: he'd never worked in the field.

He didn't understand what it was like simply because he *couldn't* understand.

"Anything else?" She asked, cutting off any further commentary.

"Don't forget the Seal. If you can bring it home—"

"Try to steal a priceless artefact from a bunch of sociopaths without putting myself in danger. When you put it like that, walk in the park."

Lethe was silent.

"What is it?"

"I found something...a web post. It's going viral. Can you get online?"

"Not sure what the connection's like out here. Just summarise it for me."

"Well, it's best if you just watch for yourself. I don't want to influence your interpretation."

"Oh for Christ's sake..."

There was a pile of oil drums about thirty metres away. They'd provide good cover. Then she could watch whatever it was that had Jude's panties in a wad. "Send it to me."

She broke cover, scurrying towards the drums.

Behind them were the remains of an old jeep. Its rear axle was supported on concrete blocks. The gap between the drums and the jeep was enough—barely—to provide a hiding place. She hunkered down and pulled her phone out of her pocket. The signal was weak, but it hadn't deteriorated to the Edge network or plain 2G, meaning she had a data connection. She clicked on the link Lethe sent to her.

General Yussef Saddiq—in full dress uniform—looked back at her from the small screen. She could barely hear his heavily accented English, but she couldn't risk turning it up. This wasn't for his followers. This was propaganda. A message for the whole world.

"Believers of the world, I bring you a warning. The time is at hand. Allah's vengeance will be felt in the heart of every infidel who has kept his holy places out of the reach of the devoted. He has delivered to me the weapon. And with that weapon I shall strike them down."

He held up his hand. On his palm was a small, battered, gold ring. The Seal of Solomon. Orla paused the video. It was the same ring they'd seen on the screens back in Nonesuch.

"This is the Seal of Solomon," Saddiq said when she hit "play". He was utterly calm. Focused. "This is the weapon. This will bring the enemies of Islam to their knees. This will drive them from the land that is rightfully ours. Tomorrow, the world will feel the power of the ring for the first time in thousands of years. Tomorrow, when the world is watching, we shall usher in the End of Days."

His image remained on the screen for a moment after he had finished speaking. The single frame showed his piercing eyes.

"Okay," she said. "I've seen it. What are the Israelis saying about it?"

"There are calls from the public for the army to track down Saddiq and bring him to justice. Some are demanding it for their own safety, but they are in the minority. His possession of such a rare and precious part of their cultural identity is an affront. It doesn't matter that the two faiths share an early history. They want it back, just like the old man predicted. When your part of the world wakes, the shit's really going to hit the fan."

"The Americans?"

"On high alert. They have a carrier moving towards the Gulf."

"No one on the ground?"

"Not that we can tell from here, but that doesn't mean they don't have someone in place. But I think it's safe to assume you're the only one who can make a difference right now."

"Understood."

"The only consolation is that the Israelis don't know where Saddiq is. If they did, they'd be sending the troops in right now."

"And then it'd get ugly," she said.

The men inside the building must have known there would be people looking for Saddiq. It was safe to assume there was already a significant price on his head. When daylight came, they'd be on their guard. Right now, they still thought they were off the grid.

Things were changing quickly.

The next few hours were going to be crucial.

But that didn't change anything for her. She was on the ground. It was close to midnight. The clock was ticking.

And she still wanted the Beast dead.

TWENTY-ONE

The LED light on the alarm clock showed 11.55.

Konstantin had itchy feet.

Figuratively and literally. He was sharing his bed with bugs. They came out when it was dark. He'd burn his clothes when he got home. Right now, he was having trouble with the fact that there were people out there who needed his help and he was reduced to being a bedbug snack.

"Lethe?" he said, triggering the ear bud.

There was a pause for a moment. He could hear Lethe's breathing on the line so he knew he was there.

"Can't sleep?" Konstantin asked the silence.

"I'll sleep when it's all over and you're all home. What can I do for you, big guy?"

"Tell me how to find Orla."

"No can do. The old man would have my bollocks on a plate."

"What do you think I'll do if something happens to her?"

"Kill half of Palestine."

"So, tell me where she is."

"I can only tell you what the boss' orders are."

"You won't help?"

"I didn't say that. Your job is to back her up if she can't deal with the bomb, and if you feel she can't, for whatever reason, then who am I to argue with you?"

"I think you just saved a life."

"My own, probably." Lethe said. Konstantin didn't argue with his reasoning.

"The border is open. Even the crossing guards have been stood down. You're going to have a clean run through."

"Don't tell her I'm on my way. Don't give her a chance to object or tell you she can handle things."

He killed the connection.

He retrieved a couple of items from his pack, and then checked the Glock. He stripped it and reassembled it in three minutes flat. Every pin, every spring perfect. It wouldn't let him down.

And that was good, because he was going to need it before the night was out.

*　*　*

The night felt strangely cool after the heat of the day.

The chain-smoker was gone.

Konstantin was glad, but surprised that the man had taken the hint.

Glad because it meant the man didn't have to hurt him to prevent him from letting his paymasters know he was on the move. Surprised, because in his place, he would have followed him all the way onto the plane.

Konstantin had to walk a couple of streets before he found a parked van that suited his purpose.

He would rather have had something more suited to the rough terrain out beyond the city limits, but beggars couldn't be choosers.

Before he could jimmy the lock, a pair of headlights swung around the corner and crawled towards him.

The car slowed, stopping as it drew level with him.

The window rolled down, and a familiar, grinning face looked out at him.

"Hey, Yankee. I thought it was you! Need a ride?"

"Don't you ever sleep?"

"Of course. I sleep plenty. But I try to do it when the tourists are drunk, so I don't have to worry about them. Besides, I can charge double after midnight, so you fancy making me a rich man? Kiddies need new shoes," he said with a grin.

Konstantin looked at him.

He didn't like the idea of getting a civilian involved.

He looked at his watch. Almost thirty minutes after midnight. "Okay, take me into Palestine."

"Palestine? Oh no, my friend. No one goes over now. It's like the Twilight Zone. A dead place. Let me take you to another girl, eh? I will come back and get you in the morning, we'll be the first over the border."

"It's open," Konstantin said.

"No. Always closed."

"It's open," Konstantin repeated.

The taxi driver looked at him and realised he was serious.

"Are you serious?"

"I am always serious."

The taxi driver understood the implications of free movement in and out of Israel. He wasn't thinking about free trade or ramping up the fares. He was local. He lived with the permanent threat of violence hanging over his head. He drove down streets knowing that he was always a target for one side or another. No, he wasn't thinking about cashing in:

he was thinking about the reality of what no one standing guard between here and Palestine meant.

"I should charge more; double. Treble," he said, shaking his head. For the first time he could remember, the driver wasn't smiling.

"I could buy your cab for that."

"You could. And I might just let you. Going in there now. Not good, Yankee. Even if you are James Bond. Dollars only. Two hundred for the night."

Konstantin slid into the back seat and took four notes from his wallet. Crisp hundred dollar bills. He reached over to the driver.

The man shook his head, "Too much. Two hundred, and I am already ripping you off mercilessly."

"Four hundred, two hundred bonus for not getting us killed. It's a fair price for what we're about to do."

"Is it too late to drop you off at the whorehouse?"

"Afraid so."

"Remind me not to pick up any more Americans, eh?"

"With pleasure; but I'd avoid the Russians, too."

"Russian?"

"Not anymore," Konstantin said. "Time to go."

He swiped the touchscreen on his phone, and a few fingertip-touches later he could see that Lethe had got the tracking device uplinked to his GPS system. He could see exactly where the Land Rover was. Lethe had texted directions to the compound too, in case the phone link went down.

They crept through the abandoned checkpoint at barely five miles an hour, the driver expecting to be challenged.

The cabins were empty, the safety glass reflecting the moon.

Konstantin studied the taxi driver through the mirror. The man was obviously uncomfortable. He was shuffling in his seat. The beads on his seat cover rubbed against one another each time he moved. But he kept on driving straight ahead.

It didn't take long for them to leave the houses behind.

In the absence of any kind of streetlights, the driver maintained a steady fifty, even though the road surface was treacherously uneven and the headlights weren't picking up the edge of the road.

Ideally, they would have gone in dark, but Konstantin didn't think asking the driver to kill the headlights would have gone down too well, even with four hundred bucks still warm in his back pocket.

Stupidity was like heroism: it didn't have a price.

He checked the icon on the screen. It wasn't moving. The road curved slightly to the right, according to the map.

He spotted the track.

He told the driver to pull over before the turning onto the dusty track that led down to the compound.

"Strange place to get dropped off," he said. "You being picked up by the mother ship?"

"Something like that," Konstantin said, reaching for the door handle.

"You need me to stick around?"

"Mother ship, remember?" He mimed flying out of there.

The driver laughed. "Take care, my crazy friend."

Konstantin climbed out of the car. He watched as it turned around and headed back the way they had come. He didn't move until it was out of sight.

He felt for the reassuring presence of the Glock.

He closed his fist around it.

And then he jogged slowly down the middle of the dirt track.

TWENTY-TWO

The sound seemed impossibly loud.

Orla tried to work in the dark.

It wasn't easy.

Every movement caused the smallest stone to move, every adjustment, no matter how slight, caused a single squeak, every uneven breath as she struggled with it was amplified in the silence of the night.

As plans went it was piss poor, unlikely to work, and even if it did, the damage would be limited at best.

She hoped the light was poor enough to mask her tampering.

There wasn't much more she could do without giving herself away. But maybe it had come to that? The bomb, she hoped, was neutralised. And if it wasn't, she'd bought Frost some time. She was assuming it'd be a remote detonation, but there was nothing to say the driver wouldn't be some willing zealot, ready to die for his cause.

And giving away her presence meant risking the enemy realising that she'd tampered with the Land Rover.

But...maybe she could use that to her advantage?

Her mind was racing.

The old van was close by. The original metal fuel cap had been replaced with a plastic one. There was rust around the cap itself, but no lock. She hoped the tank was full.

The petrol cap turned smoothly in her hand. She was hit by the unmistakeable odour of diesel fumes as it came off. It was wet and sticky.

She moved quickly, pulling a T-shirt from her rucksack. She tore it into strips and started to push the strips far enough into the tank for the material to begin soaking up the fuel.

It didn't take long before the fumes were overpowering.

Orla took a step back to clear the heaviness from her head.

She fumbled inside her bag again, fishing out a book of matches. They had the name of a bar she could no longer remember stamped onto the cover in gold foil. She couldn't even remember which city it was in. That was what her life was like: always moving, never staying in the same place long enough to see and understand, to get to grips with the intricacies of the culture and the people. It was all surface level now, shallow.

She lit the end of the fuel-soak rag and took cover.

She had barely hidden herself behind a pile of broken rocks before the van exploded in noise and flame, twisted metal spinning through the air, glass raining down. The night was filled with blazing light and billowing smoke and the terrible silence that followed the destructive rage of the explosion.

Moments later she heard voices.

The men poured out of the building.

The first man ignored the blaze completely. He sprinted toward the Land Rover. They might as well have painted a big sign on the vehicle. A couple of seconds later, he was inside and moving it to make sure the fire couldn't spread to it. It was all the confirmation Orla needed.

The spit of fire and the twisting shriek of metal from the blazing van, coupled with the sudden roar of the Land Rover's engine as the driver put his foot to the floor, masked the sound of Orla's first shot.

Across the compound's yard, directly parallel with the main door, one of the men stumbled and fell. He didn't make a sound. He didn't have time to. The bullet from Orla's Jericho 941 tore out his throat.

In that endless moment, none of Saddiq's crew seemed to understand that there was a danger in the night.

She fired again.

The bastard got lucky. Just as she squeezed down on the trigger, he turned his ankle on a stone and twisted. The bullet ricocheted off the stone wall behind him. It missed him by less than quarter of an inch. He must have felt the wind as it whistled past him. He cried out, and a retaliatory shot was fired in her general direction. It was wild and wide, and buried itself into the side of corrugated iron of the door ten yards away from her hiding place.

No one made any sort of attempt to put out the blaze.

It was far enough from the main building and the bomb-car that it didn't pose a threat.

No, their focus was on dealing with the real threat: her.

Two of Saddiq's men dived inside the building again, taking cover. The Land Rover's driver ran head-down towards safety.

She took another shot.

He screamed and twisted and stumbled, but rose to his feet again clutching his arm, and disappeared inside.

He was still alive, which meant he was still dangerous. She could try to keep them pinned inside, but she wasn't sure how long that could work. They'd almost certainly send someone out the back to try and flank her in the dark.

She didn't have time to worry about it.

She heard the sound of breaking glass as the butt of a rifle shattered a window. Orla fired a shot, blind. It wasn't about hitting the shooter; she just wanted him cautious. She ducked down again, checking the clip. She had one spare. But that still meant more than twenty rounds. Two dead, one injured. That left three uninjured men for her to deal with, one of them the Beast. Four hostiles to take out in total. Five rounds apiece. She was going to have to be a little more selective with the shots she took.

The crack of a rifle shot rang out from the house.

The bullet hit one of the rocks beside her.

It could have been a lucky shot—or the shooter might have some decent kit, a night sight.

Another shot zinged in, too close for comfort.

She needed to move, and move quickly, before they pinned her down.

She couldn't afford to become a sitting duck.

She cursed the moon.

Even a little cloud would have doubled her chances of moving undetected.

Any kind of movement was risky.

But she couldn't just sit tight and wait for the bastards to pick her off, either.

She pressed her hands against the dirt, like a sprinter waiting for the gun, and as the next shot rang out, she burst into action, sprinting hard, arms and legs pumping furiously as she did. She held the Jericho out to the side and squeezed off a single shot in the general direction of the open window. It pinged off the concrete and cinder block. The sniper didn't return fire. She made it to the stack of barrels. She ducked down behind them. One of them rocked as she leaned against it. She felt the swill of liquid inside it, but was there enough to be of any use?

A quick glance back to the house revealed the muzzle flash of the sniper's next shot.

The bullet tore into the rocks where she had been hidden only seconds ago.

The shooter thought she was still there.

Now she could only hope that would give herself long enough to do something.

The van was still burning, but the flames had already begun to die down. Great gulfs of black smoke still billowed out of the wreckage, though. She could use that. She could move so that the smoke—which wasn't dispersing quickly, because there was next to no wind—was between her and the shooter. Then she could risk getting closer.

She knew that her only chance was to get inside the building; otherwise they could just wait it out and pick her off as the sun came up. The clock was against her, just like the rest of the odds.

She didn't have a choice.

Not really.

Orla ran because her life depended on it.

She managed five long strides before the gunfire started again.

She made it into cover.

She only needed another few yards and the smoke and the burning van would give her the protection she needed.

But the scant cover she had wasn't going to be adequate now that they knew where she was.

And so she ran again.

TWENTY-THREE

The explosion drowned out every other sound.

A moment later, a sudden tongue of flame lit the sky.

Konstantin started to run.

There was only one reason for fire: Orla was in trouble. She'd have preferred to deal with things silently. Huge explosions were not silent.

"Lethe? You hear me Lethe?" he half-shouted, anxiety creeping in the second time he was forced to ask the question, with only silence as an answer. He tapped the ear bud again and repeated the call.

Nothing.

"Shit," he said.

That was as expressive as the big Russian got.

The compound and the blazing van came into view.

Konstantin slowed, dropping to a crouch. Logically, the chances of anyone peering into the darkness and seeing him were remote; but logic didn't matter on the battlefield. It was all a matter of instinct, of muscle memory.

He drew the Glock.

He took a moment to assess the situation.

There was no way of knowing for sure who had set the van on fire, but if he was going to stake his life on it he'd bet on Orla every time.

Where was she?

He scanned the darkness.

The fire cast crazy shadows everywhere, giving the illusion of movement.

He saw a flicker of something over on the lower part of the hillside, directly opposite the compound buildings. He would have discounted it for fire-shadows but for the *crack* of gunfire from one of the building's upstairs windows.

So they knew she was out there.

Did they know where?

He cursed the fact that he had lost contact with Lethe.

He had no way to communicate directly with Orla and no way of knowing if she knew he was on his way.

The best thing he could do was make his way around to the other side of the building, while she drew their fire. He'd just have to hope she didn't mistake him for one of Saddiq's guys and start shooting at him.

A shot rang out from where she was sheltering.

He took it as a sign to get his arse into gear, and started to move.

Ten seconds later, he was out of direct line-of-sight from the window and could breathe more easily.

There was no sign of anyone outside the buildings—which, he hoped, meant the Seal was in there too.

That seriously amplified the risks.

He drew closer to the building, moving as near to silently as was humanly possible. The big man thought he saw someone lying in wait. He slowed, watching, listening, ready to make a corpse.

Still, the man didn't move.

He was either incredibly disciplined, or he was dead.

Konstantin waited.

He didn't move a muscle.

He was a night hunter.

He was lethal.

He let the shadows slither and slide around him.

He waited.

The man didn't shoot.

Konstantin moved closer.

The man didn't move. He didn't blink. The moonlight reflected in his glassy eyes. Dead.

He had been garrotted. Orla's handiwork.

There was a fairly new-looking Land Rover parked—or rather, abandoned—a short distance from the buildings and the burning van. He covered the distance quickly. The keys were still in the ignition.

He put a hand on the bonnet; it was still warm.

Good to know they had a way out, if the shit really hit the fan. He always liked to know his exit strategy.

He left the keys in the ignition—saved fumbling with them later if they needed to get out of there in a hurry.

There was more gunfire. Another staccato burst. The sound changed quality and depth as the rounds stopped tearing off the corrugated iron of the outbuilding, and hit the more solid cinder block and concrete shell of the one beside it.

Konstantin ran straight towards the burning van.

The smoke around it was thicker than the flames.

The shots came from one upstairs room, but that didn't mean that there was no-one downstairs.

He tried Lethe again. Better to get a sit rep and use all the tricks at their disposal, than go in blind.

Lethe didn't answer.

So blind it was.

TWENTY-FOUR

"Koni? Orla? Can you hear me? One of you?" The link had dropped out, and Lethe had lost them both. He worked frantically to re-establish contact, cycling through the channels, trying alternative frequencies, but there was nothing.

"*Shitfuckshitbastardbuggeringbollocks.*" He hit the side of the terminal. The satellite images were streaming through uninterrupted on to the screen in front of him. He could see the pair of them.

The initial fear that they were dead lasted only a few seconds.

They were some of the worst seconds of his life.

He felt utterly helpless.

He really didn't like that.

He pressed his right hand flat against the touch screen, and adjusted the headset with his left. "Frosty? Can you hear me?"

Silence crackled back.

He was about to scream, when Ronan Frost came back: "Loud and clear. Problem?" Frost sounded exhausted. Unsurprising, given it was the middle of the night and he'd travelled non-stop for a full day. It was forty-eight hours since he'd managed any sleep.

"Depends on your definition of the word."

"Jude?"

"Nothing for you to worry about. Just get yourself back to sleep."

"Tell me now. Tell me exactly what's got you rattled, or so help me God I'll come back to Nonesuch and smack you senseless."

"It's nothing, honestly, a technical snafu. I just wanted to check which end it was on. So no need to come home and kick my arse, thank you very much."

He broke the connection and ignored Frost's name as it flashed on his screen.

Lethe ran a full diagnostic check on the system. He did not take his eyes from the screen. He monitored the hijacked satellite feed. It was a blessing and a curse. He could see they were alive, but he was powerless to help. Logically, he knew that they were more than capable of working without his assistance; but they were a team. He was field ops back up. He kept them safe. He brought them home. And if he couldn't do that...

Confirmation came through.

There was *nothing* wrong with his equipment.

But that didn't explain why his messages weren't reaching them. There was a limit to how long the Russian would go before casting his earpiece aside in frustration. He wasn't the most patient soul. Orla was running dark, so she wouldn't even know there was a problem until it was too late.

So the man of science had to pray to a deity he didn't believe in and ask him to look after the pair of them out there until he could get his shit working again.

Almost as soon as he'd finished beseeching the invisible all-knowing one, he cracked it: someone was using an electromagnetic pulse to disrupt a whole spectrum of radio waves in a very controlled area. The area where Saddiq's dirty bomb was. Where Koni and Orla were.

The whole thing stank of military intervention—and not from the Palestinians. It was far more sophisticated than anything he would have expected from them.

It was time to wake the old man.

TWENTY-FIVE

There was only one obvious place for her to go.

Orla knew that she had already caused enough damage to delay, if not fulfil, the first of her objectives. She could probably slip away now that the immediate threat had been neutralised.

But.

There was always a "but".

The old man wanted more.

And he was right.

It wasn't enough.

It wasn't just the depleted Uranium core and the C4; it was the people with their causes that were the real threat. They weren't so easily stopped.

And one of them was personal.

The old man would understand—he was a vengeful bastard. Control had told her about what he'd done to the Dockland Bombers that put him in his wheelchair. Anyone capable of that would understand her going after the Beast. This was her one shot. He was in there. She had to take it. She wouldn't be able to live with herself if she didn't.

Orla used the burning van as a shield. She stayed as close to it as the heat allowed. It wouldn't explode again. There was nothing left to detonate. It was almost done burning. The heat was uncomfortable, the smoke thick and choking her as she breathed. She covered her nose and mouth with another strip of torn T-shirt. No shots came. Her eyes stung. They streamed with tears. It was like the last time. Everything was blurry and indistinct. She saw the open door as a dark hole in the middle of the concrete and cinderblock wall. The symbolism of the moment wasn't lost on her: it was the same door she'd run through when she'd escaped the Beast.

She wasn't the same woman, now. This time, she sprinted towards it, ready to slay the Beast.

Still, silence held court.

The men had no idea she was inside the compound building with them.

The interior was burned into her memory. Even in the darkness, she knew exactly where the corridors led, how many doors waited for her, and where the filthy mattress she had been raped repeatedly on lay.

Had other women been abused on that bed since? The thought hit her like a hammer blow. Had other women been subjected to the same brutal tortures? If they had, were they as strong as she had been, or had the Beast broken them?

Please God, let me have been the last, she thought.

She didn't need light to recognize the stale reek of sex and piss that clung to the rooms. The odours were enough to drag her back in time. Sense memory was like that. Dangerous. She blocked out the flood of feelings associated with the smells. She couldn't let them drag her back and make her a victim again. Not if she wanted to escape this place a second time.

Outside, a burst of gunfire strafed the night; automatic this time, not the single shot of a sniper rifle.

She pressed herself deeper into the shadows.

She turned to look.

Orla saw the silhouette of the man cast in stark relief against the remains of the burning van.

She raised the Jericho 941, and for a heartbeat thought about shooting. Her eyes still stung from the smoke and fumes. Just pulling the trigger would let everyone know precisely where she was; miss, and she'd have painted a target on herself a mile wide. She was trapped between the Devil she knew and the Devil she didn't, and she had to decide which offered the best chance of survival. Chance? Miss, and she had no chance at all, even if the gunman could not see her clearly. One shot. Hit or miss. Live or die.

She didn't take it.

She wanted the Beast.

The man lit by the fire wasn't the Beast.

His physique was all wrong.

His line of sight was away from the building—away from her.

He turned slightly.

Something had drawn his attention away from her.

She slowed her breathing, waiting until he presented his back to her.

She steadied the gun, blinking the astringent sting of the smoke away again. The double-tap of her heartbeat intensified. The sound swelled in the silence, becoming so loud it was the only thing she could hear.

She knew she should take the shot.

You didn't leave an enemy at your back.

She slowly increased the pressure on the trigger, moving it towards the tipping point. She would much rather have slipped out into the yard again and come up behind him with the garrotte.

She hesitated.

It could have cost her her life.

The man stepped away from the burning van, out of her line of sight. The opportunity was lost.

Orla eased the pressure on the trigger.

She lowered the Jericho.

She pressed her back up against the wall.

She had a choice: go deeper into the darkness, face her demon, slay the Beast; or she could back out, turn around, run, lose herself in the hills beyond the remnants of the refugee camp in the distance.

She wanted to run.

But she wanted to slay the Beast more.

Gunfire again. Close. For a second, she thought it was aimed at her. In that second, she stumbled sideways a step, flinching. Her foot caught something and sent it clattering across the floor.

"Throw your weapon out!" a voice tailor-made for this Hell shouted.

She would have known the voice anywhere.

It had haunted her dreams.

She could smell him now.

Close.

The Beast had her cornered.

She didn't answer.

Her hand tightened around the Jericho's grip.

Just because he'd called out, didn't mean he knew where she was.

The dark was endless.

She saw the barrel of his gun, lit by the short burst of fire that erupted from it.

He wasn't shooting at her, was he?

Bullets tore into the cinderblock lining of the building wall. Nowhere near her hiding place.

Orla crouched, slipping slowly down the wall, her back always pressed up against the cold bricks.

Was he trying to reach for the handle and close the door, trapping her inside the cell?

Orla fired wildly, again and again until the Jericho *clicked* empty.

She had a second clip. She could load the gun blindfold. But she fumbled it in the dark. The clip clattered to the floor.

It was too dark to see where it fell.

She reached out, patting the floor, trying to find it, blind.

She had an empty gun and the Beast was at the door.

TWENTY-SIX

Still nothing.

Lethe had to be as frustrated as Konstantin was, but that didn't help him now. Now. Here. He needed comms up. A team lived and died by communication in combat scenarios. He was effectively deaf and blind. Lethe would be doing everything he could, frantically trying to find other channels, bouncing his signal off some satellite relay or whatever it was he did, but it didn't matter. There were still parts of the earth that were black spots; places so remote that phone coverage was out; places where the geographical features neutralised the cell phone towers. Places, in other words, where digital communication was impossible.

But all of that technology was a luxury the Russian had lived without before, and would happily live without again. It made them soft. They lost their edge because they expected the voice in their ear to whisper what to do.

He pulled out the ear-bud and slipped it into his pocket. He wanted to hear what the world had to tell him. He didn't need guiding, like some character in a computer game. Time to rely on flesh and blood, and trust his senses. He waited a moment, letting himself attune to the surroundings: the crackle of the burning van and the blistering paintwork, the whistle of the wind and the creek of the corrugated iron doors of the barn, and the sheer quiet that encompassed it all.

He saw someone moving through the firelight from the van.

Using the smoke as a shield, the figure disappeared into the building.

It was slight—feminine?

It didn't move like a man, the Russian thought, but there was no way of knowing for sure.

A second figure emerged from another door—bigger, more masculine.

It started to make its way along the side of the building, towards the door where the first had disappeared.

The first one was Orla. Had to be.

And that meant she was in trouble.

He had to get inside, take the man out, and do it without alerting the terrorists to his presence—which meant keeping Orla in the dark, too.

The guard had suffered a swift death; the clear wire grooves across his throat were testimony to that. Konstantin checked his body. He wore a holster. It was empty. So Orla had a gun again. That was something. There was no telling how much ammo he'd had on him—maybe a second clip, if he was the cautious sort. Maybe not.

The Russian had an idea how he could draw fire from the building, and maybe buy Orla a little time without her knowing he was there. It was even environmental... it involved recycling the corpse.

TWENTY-SEVEN

"I hope this is good, Mr Lethe." The old man was like some sort of vampire—he never seemed to sleep.

Lethe closed the door behind him. "Not good. Bad. Very bad, actually. I think."

"Why don't you spit it out before I die of old age?"

"I lost contact with Orla and Konstantin. I thought it was just some sort of blackout, satellite rotation, something; hell, even just clogged traffic on the network. It's not. Someone's jamming the frequency."

"Are you sure?"

"Absolutely."

"It couldn't just be the terrain?"

Lethe shook his head. "Nope. I've tried rerouting through a couple of alternative satellites, I've piggybacked an Israeli feed and a US one, nothing."

"But you're still getting pictures?"

Lethe nodded. "Which is what tipped me off. The jammer is pretty bloody primitive. Maybe even just a cell phone jammer. It's not exactly revolutionary stuff: you can pick them up at most electronics stores, if you know what you're looking for. Most are short range. There was a case not so long ago about a guy using it on the bus during his daily commute, because he was fed up of all the noise. This is bigger, but it's the same principle. It's the kind of thing the FBI use in takedowns to isolate the target."

"Could the Palestinians be operating it?"

"Why would they want to? It isolates them, too."

"Indeed."

Lethe went over to the old man's computer and called up the feed from his own terminal downstairs.

"I was recording this when the signal dropped out," he jabbed a finger at the main building in the complex. He started the recording. The face of the General appeared, the ring on his finger, talking animatedly into the camera. "They were live-streaming it from the compound. The blackout took the stream down, which makes me think someone else has them on lockdown. I've not been able to get it translated yet, but Saddiq's not happy."

The clip ended after little more than a minute, the screen going suddenly white.

"Whoever's jamming them knew where to look. A minute's not long enough to trace and isolate a feed, no matter how good you are. This stuff takes time. And like I said, there's no way Saddiq and his mob would want to jam their own broadcast while their glorious leader was in full flow."

The old man sat silently for a moment.

"So who's doing it?"

"There's only one answer that makes any kind of sense to me," Lethe said. "The Israelis."

The old man nodded. "Sometimes, I hate my life. Whatever it is they're doing, find a way to beat it. Those are our people down there."

TWENTY-EIGHT

She was trapped.

There was only one way in and out of this room.

That was why they'd used it as a cell.

The door bolted from the outside—that was a relic of its previous incarnation, too.

It was out of her hands.

– She'd have to wait until the door opened again.

And it would.

They didn't know she was in here.

More gunfire erupted outside.

That stopped Orla cold.

It made no sense at all.

Unless...

They thought she wasn't alone.

So either they were shooting blindly into the darkness— which would burn through ammunition. Not that they'd ever run out. The compound was a training centre. She'd always known that was what it was, even when it was side-by- side with the refugee camp and filled to overcrowding with desperate, tired, hungry people. Jihadists had hidden in their midst, using them as cover.

She had spent enough time around guns to differentiate weapons by the sound of their fire—at least basic types. One was a handgun being fired from a distance, another was a rifle—sniper rifle, she assumed—being fired from the upstairs window. The third was a submachine gun.

And all three were firing now.

Orla moved closer to the door. The gunfire masked any noise she made. She couldn't see anything and she couldn't hear anything else. It just put as much distance as possible between her and the mattress bundled in the corner of the cell.

The mattress.

Mercifully, the darkness hid any bloodstains that had ingrained themselves into the floor from the Boy.

The mattress.

It wouldn't be an effective barrier against a handgun, never mind a submachine gun. The bullets would tear through it, and through her behind it. But it might hide her just a moment longer. And that moment might make the difference.

She waited, breathing the stale air.

The stinks on it hadn't changed.

They had seeped into the stone.

She could taste them on her tongue.

The taste brought with it a moment of pain, a moment of fear, and finally, a moment of vengeance.

She had lived through the pain and the fear.

Not the vengeance.

Not yet.

And "yet" was the most powerful word she knew.

She would have her revenge tonight, even if she died making it happen.

She couldn't have the Beast and Jenin hanging over her for the rest of her life. Now she knew that he had survived, she had to do something. She couldn't let him prey on others. That would be worse than having died in this cell all those years ago.

She wedged the mattress up, making it look as though she was hiding behind it.

Then she moved over to the wall beside the door and stood with her back pressed against it. She couldn't see the door or the corridor beyond it anymore. It didn't matter. The Beast would come to her.

The shooting stopped.

Orla held her breath.

The door opened—only a little, but the ambient light from the still-burning van stole into the cell, as bright as any spotlight. There was a burst of gunfire and the mattress bled feathers as bullet after bullet shredded it. The Beast unloaded a full clip into it.

He stepped inside.

There was an arrogance to the way he moved.

He was so sure that Orla was dead or dying behind the mattress.

"Surprise," she whispered in his ear as she looped the wire of the garrotte over his head.

His hand was inside the loop before she pulled it tight.

The wire sliced into his flesh.

He cried out, choking but fighting it, and she knew she'd screwed up. She shouldn't have said a thing. She should have just killed him. But she had wanted him to know that it was her. She had wanted hers to be the last voice he heard. And it had cost her. She was strong, but he was stronger. She pulled savagely on the garrotte, but even as it bit further into his hand, she knew it wouldn't be enough to disable him.

But it would ruin his hand.

That might—just might—save her life if he broke free.

She refused to let go.

She drew the wire even tighter until he dropped the gun.

He used his free hand to reach behind him and grab for Orla's hair.

He tangled his fist into a handful of it, and yanked down hard.

She gasped and cried out with pain, but refused to loosen her grip, pulling tighter instead.

"I've come back to kill you," she goaded, using all the hatred she had harboured for the Beast to give her strength. "Do you remember me?"

The Beast laughed.

TWENTY-NINE

Konstantin watched the man close the door.

Orla was inside.

Trapped.

He dragged the corpse across the ground. It was slow going. Slower than he would have liked. He had to stop every few yards and wait, letting the sounds settle, so that he could move on again. He'd seen a pile of broken stones that would serve his purpose; they were close enough to provide better, more substantial cover than anything else he would be able to reach before all hell broke loose.

He propped the body up in the sitting position. It wasn't particularly convincing, but given the darkness and the fact that they'd be under fire, it would do. Illusions didn't have to be perfect. And this one just had to fool a few people for a few minutes.

He waited. Listened to the sounds of the world around him. He wasn't a believer in sixth senses, or preternatural grace, or whatever nonsense it was those paperback writers liked to call it. He believed in instinct. He believed in training.

But more importantly, Konstantin Khavin believed in himself.

He fired a single shot in the direction of the man he could see silhouetted through the doorway, and then dived for cover.

One.

Two.

And on three, the night air was full of the sound of gunfire.

Both men—the silhouette in the doorway and the sniper in the window—riddled the corpse with bullets.

The plan was simple—misdirection. While their attention was on the dead guard, Konstantin made his move. He wanted to get into a position where he could help Orla. But that wasn't going to be easy, and given the choice, he would much rather not have tipped his hand and let them know there was someone else involved. But beggars couldn't be choosers. So they knew he was out there? So what? It wouldn't help their life expectancy. And if they were as undisciplined as they seemed to be, they wouldn't check the corpse, so the chances were, they'd think he was dead and would be busy high-fiving themselves as he cut their throats.

He ran, using the still burning van as his shield.

It masked his movement.

Konstantin kept his distance from the flames, letting the smoke cover him. He could still feel the searing heat against his face.

The gunfire stopped.

He was exposed—in the no man's land between the cover of the barrels and the outbuildings. The only thing stopping him from being lit up like Guy Fawkes was the fact that the smoke was thick enough and black enough to hide him from the moon. Even so, the flames were bright. All it would take was one of the men to look his way, and he was screwed.

He flinched instinctively.

It was different—it echoed differently. It was coming from inside the building, but deep inside, rather than from the doorway.

Konstantin watched the man turn and disappear back inside.

He had a moment when he could have taken the shot, but before he could, he heard a sudden cry of pain that put a smile on his lips. Orla had just turned the odds in their favour. She was more than capable of taking care of herself. He turned his attention to the sniper. He needed to get inside, take the man by surprise. Given what had just gone down, the best way to play it was naturally, act like he owned the place, just walk in and let them think he was one of them, returning from the kill.

Another shot rang out from the upstairs window.

The corpse wobbled, but like a Weeble it didn't fall down.

Konstantin hurried around the remains of the van and across the empty ground to the building's wall, Glock raised, ready.

He took a second to regulate his breathing, to listen to the darkness beyond the doorway, and then pushed away from the wall. He stood in the doorway. He didn't want to distract Orla, but he didn't want her plugging him full of lead, either. She would, if she thought he was one of Saddiq's crew.

He entered the building.

He moved quickly down the corridor, until he reached the first door.

He didn't stop.

He didn't even glance into the darkness.

He moved on, just another shadow.

He walked to the end of the corridor. A door blocked his entry into the main house. He waited, listening. No challenge came. He pushed open the door and stepped into an empty hallway. There were more doors. The one to his left was open. There was no one inside. There was a table in the door to his right, with the remains of several half-eaten meals going cold on their plates.

Ahead rose a short flight of wooden stairs. The boards were bare. There was no carpeting to cushion the sound of his footsteps.

He could hear voices above him.

THIRTY

The Beast flung his head back, slamming it into the bridge of her nose with a sickening crack.

Orla's world threatened to turn black.

No matter how hard she tried, she couldn't maintain her grip on the wooden pegs at the ends of her garrotte. They were slick with blood from the Beast's fingers. But even as they slipped through her fingers, she still knew the wire had bitten deep into his flesh—deep enough that it would remain embedded without her weight pulling it tight.

Blood erupted from her nose.

It was broken.

Blood and snot bubbled as her breathing quickened.

She fell back to the ground, landing on the gun that he'd dropped. The muzzle dug into her spine. It was more painful than the blow to her face. She had to move quickly, despite the pain. If he pinned her down, she wouldn't get back up again. It wasn't going to be a best-out-of-three contest.

Orla threw herself to one side. The Beast lashed out, swinging a wild kick at her.

His boot still caught her. It was a glancing blow, but it was still painful as it drove into her ribs. Only the fact that she was moving away from it stopped it from breaking three or four of the bones.

He towered over her.

And then he came down, looming over her, his face in hers as he sneered.

She could taste the stench of his breath.

He stared at her with his one good eye.

She couldn't crawl out of the way fast enough.

She grabbed for the gun she had been lying on and swung it with every ounce of strength and hatred she had in her. The butt of the pistol grip *cracked* against the side of his head.

It didn't stop him.

He was a demon.

Rage drove out all feeling.

She'd fought men like him before.

She had to kill him. Nothing else would slow him down.

The Beast fell on top of her. He grabbed at her wrists, pinning her down. He slammed his arse down on her chest, driving the air out of her lungs. The gun spun away, lost.

Orla struggled to breathe in with his weight pressing down on her.

Blood dripped from his throat and onto her face.

She clenched her teeth. She refused to open her mouth, no matter how desperately she wanted to breathe. She wasn't taking any of his blood into her.

"You," the Beast said. "I should have recognised the stink coming from between your legs." The Beast cursed her, but it was clear that it *hurt* to talk. The wire of the garrotte was still wedged close to his vocal cords.

He followed the direction of her eyes.

He knew what she was looking at.

He pulled the wire free with one hand and he held it above her face. It didn't come all the way out of the new smile it had opened beneath his chin. The blood flowed all the more freely, though. "You are going to die in this room," he said. "It is your destiny. This room is where the world ends. I told you that the last time you were here. And now it is true. Destiny is inescapable."

He hit her across the face with his bloody fist.

Orla felt the familiar blackness creeping up on her.

This time it was different, though.

This time, she would rather die than become a prisoner.

And that meant she had nothing to lose.

If she was going to die, then she was going to die on her own terms.

With one arm pinned beneath the Beast, Orla reached up with her free hand, and clawed at his face. She tore at the skin with her nails, ripping the eye patch off.

The Beast tried to grab her hand and pull it away from his face, but as he did, her fingers caught on one of the garrotte pegs.

It was the force of his own movement that ripped it from his flesh.

He screamed and rolled away from her, clutching at his throat. Blood pulsed through his fingers.

He had done more damage to his throat than she could possibly have hoped.

The wire had nicked one of the major arteries.

There was no coming back from that.

Orla rolled out from beneath him.

Her instinct was to run for the doorway—but this time, she was seeing it through to the end. No regrets. No wondering if he was still out there.

The Beast was on his feet somehow, stumbling towards her.

He refused to die.

Orla met him head on, straight-armed, her palms slamming into his chest. The impact toppled the Beast. He sprawled onto the mattress where he'd raped her again and again; where the Boy had cradled her in his arms, weeping; where her innocence had died. And where, finally, the Beast would die.

She levelled a boot at his head, bending it like Beckham. She drove her foot full into his face and it felt *good*.

She tried to remember all the anger, all the rage, and beneath it, the driving fear she had buried for so long, and used it to fight through her own pain.

Her foot kicked her empty gun—it could have been his. She'd lost track. She didn't care. She reached down for it and used it like a club, slamming it into the Beast's leering face until he stopped trying to defend himself.

She dropped the bloody gun.

She stood over him, and then she drove her heel down into the middle of his face one more time. She felt the sickening crunch as her boot caved in the front of his skull.

It was over.

She dropped the gun and turned to see a silhouette in the doorway: a man.

A man who pointed a gun at her.

She held up her hands in supplication, it was over. It didn't matter. The Beast was dead. She'd done her part. The van was burning, the explosives in the rubber tyre had been neutralised.

She could die now.

Orla Nyrén held her hands above her head and waited for the gunman to fire.

THIRTY-ONE

Konstantin had expected more resistance.

He followed the voices to the upstairs room. There were three men. One wounded. The sniper was armed, but the rifle was useless in close quarters.

Konstantin took him out with two bullets to the back and side of the head as he tried to bring the rifle around. It fell out of dead hands, landing on the hard-packed dirt two storeys below. His third shot finished the wounded man—taking him in the forehead. He hadn't managed to get half way out of the chair he'd slumped in.

Konstantin recognised the dead man. He'd been his tail from the airport. The man who'd brought the artefact to this place. Nasri.

General Youssef Saddiq was the last man.

There was no panic on his face as his companions fell. He made no attempt to reach for a weapon.

"Do you really think that you can stop me?" he asked quite calmly.

The Russian said nothing.

"I have the ultimate weapon."

He held up a hand to show Konstantin the ring—Solomon's Seal—that was the cause of the conflict here tonight. Without it, then any bomb was just that: a bomb. It was a local matter, no matter how tragic for the families who lost their lives, no matter how many fell on the wrong side of the scales when judgement was weighed out. With the ring, one country would attack another, and it would escalate. And eventually the Americans or the United Nations or maybe even the Russians would step in to end the chaos, if only to ensure the world's supply of oil wasn't threatened. It wasn't holy, unless your god was the almighty dollar.

But the symbol on the man's finger made sure that it was about more than that.

Saddiq looked at him. He didn't look insane. He held up the Seal. "With this, I can summon demons, and command the beasts of the field."

"No, you can't," Konstantin said. There was no negotiating with a madman.

Outside he heard the sound of an engine starting up and a vehicle driving away.

The Land Rover.

He should have taken the keys from it when he had the chance.

It was too late to worry about that.

"Can't I?" Saddiq laughed. "I have just sent death and destruction into the heart of Israel. You come in here with your guns, you fight and you kill, but you can't stop me. I have sent a message to the world. And the world will listen. That is the wonder of the internet."

Still keeping the Glock trained on the General, Konstantin crossed the room to the corpse slumped up against the window ledge. The bare floorboards groaned under his weight.

He had expected it to be the driver, or in the worst case, the chain smoker, but it was neither.

He had never seen the man before.

Which meant there was at least one man unaccounted for. The driver.

The bomb was on its way over the border.

Saddiq hadn't tried to escape. He could have. Instead, he sat in the chair recently vacated by the second dead man. He looked content. Harmless. Konstantin wasn't about to believe that. He walked over to where the General sat and put a single bullet through his kneecap.

The man howled in pain, clutching at his knee.

He tried to stand, which was the worst thing he could possibly have done. His leg buckled beneath him. Saddiq reached out for the wall to stop himself from falling.

"Just sit down," Konstantin barked, but the General wasn't used to taking orders.

He gripped the doorframe, then lurched sideways. For a moment Konstantin thought he was going to try and return to the chair, but as his leg gave way beneath him again, he staggered backwards, out of the room.

Konstantin reached the doorway in time to see Saddiq clutching the golden ring and beseeching whatever magic he believed it possessed to heal his ruined knee. For a moment, as the madman grinned at him, Konstantin actually believed the bastard had healed himself. He walked, one step, two steps, head held high; and then the reality of his shattered kneecap superseded any miraculously imagined healing powers the battered old ring might have had. He lost his footing at the head of the narrow staircase.

He looked at Konstantin, hate blazing in his eyes.

And then he fell.

Even from the top of the stairs, Konstantin could see from the unnatural angle he lay at that Saddiq had broken his neck on the way down.

He wouldn't be commanding any demons, now.

Konstantin breathed deeply. Inhaled. Exhaled. His part in this was over.

He took the stairs quickly, the Glock still leading the way in case of surprises.

He crouched down beside Saddiq's corpse to make sure he wasn't breathing, and then pulled the ring from the dead man's finger.

He had just slipped it inside his pocket when he registered the shape in the doorway, and heard a familiar voice calling his name.

THIRTY-TWO

There was no bullet.

"Up, quickly," the stranger said to Orla. "We need to move."

"Who are you?" she asked.

"No time for questions. We need to get your friend and get out of here. The others are on the move."

Others?

Friend?

She had no friends in the place.

The man motioned with his gun—another Jericho, she realised—for her to follow.

She took one last glance at the corpse. It wasn't the Beast anymore. It was as though death had robbed him of all of his power over her. Stripped him of the mask of tyranny. Now it was just Salem Bashar. Remembering his name didn't scare her, now. He would forever be this. A body. He wouldn't live in her dreams anymore.

She was free of him.

Smoke was pouring out of the van. The flames, dampened as they were, were still bright enough to banish the darkness. The sound of its burning had masked another sound. She caught it this time, in the distance: the sound of an engine. A car being driven away in a hurry.

Someone had managed to get out.

There was no sign of the Land Rover.

Meaning the bomb was on the move.

She'd done what she could to disable it, but that didn't mean the threat was over. She needed to get word to Lethe, but her ear-bud was silent.

She pressed it again. "Jude, you holding out on me, pretty boy?"

The stranger looked at her, confused. Then seemed to shrug as though to say 'Crazy Brits,' and walked on.

Lethe didn't answer.

She missed his endless chatter—which she never would admit to another soul. It wasn't distracting. It was reassuring. He was always there. The one constant in her life.

Only now, he wasn't.

The stranger took a military band radio from a clip at his hip and spoke into it; fast, Arabic, not one of her better languages, but she caught enough to know he was giving a sit rep back to his own version of Lethe. The voice crackled back. She heard the number five.

Lethe had said five, too, when she'd asked him how many were inside the compound buildings. One outside, five inside. But that didn't make sense. Saddiq. The Beast. The sniper. The guard she'd garrotted on the way in. The smoker she'd taken out before going inside. The guy she'd clipped. Nasri, the guy who'd brought the Seal in. That was seven. Lethe wouldn't have missed one. That was sloppy. No. The fact his number was off meant they had a shielded room in there. Probably where Saddiq was broadcasting from.

"Shit," she said.

The light from the burning van was enough to confirm the stranger was an Arab.

He carried himself like a combat vet. His Jericho was held as though it was an extension of his arm.

"There's a hidden room," she whispered.

He looked at her.

"I came in hot—my Intel said six men, five inside, one out. I count seven hostiles on site, not including you, which means at least eight live bodies when I hit the ground. They've got a shielded room. Something that stops our tech picking them up. It's the only thing that makes sense."

The man thought about it for a split second, and then spoke in rapid-fire Arabic into his radio. Static crackled back, followed by his handler. He obviously didn't like what he was hearing.

"I'm glad you went to a good school," he said. "Mathematics was never my thing."

"So I'm right?"

"We're still picking up movement inside. More than one life source. So you are right. Your friend's in there. That still leaves one unknown."

"I don't have any friends here."

"Back-up, then."

Did he mean Konstantin?

Inside?

He was meant to be on the other side of the border waiting for the bomb.

The old man had given him orders.

There was no way he'd disobey them.

But the old man had given him other orders first: to keep her safe.

Damn it.

She was through the door before the Arab could stop her.

He followed her in.

She saw Konstantin crouched over a prone body on the floor.

Orla recognised the full military regalia. Saddiq.

Konstantin looked up at her.

She could smell something. Something different. It hadn't been here before.

It took her a moment to place the smell: cigarette smoke.

And then she saw it: the glint as metal caught the flickering flame of the van. A knife. That made sense. The lurker was just inside the doorway that led to the kitchens. A little further in, and the light would never have carried. But sometimes it was better to be lucky than good.

He came rushing out of the doorway, knife slashing down toward the big Russian's shoulder and neck.

Before she could react, the Arab fired over her shoulder.

It was a clean shot. It took the chain smoker in the cheek and punched a hole out through the back of his throat.

He was dead before he hit the floor.

The knife spun away, clattering on the bare boards beside Konstantin.

The big Russian didn't so much as flinch. He turned to look at the dead man and said calmly, "I told you to go home. Why didn't you listen to me?"

The dead man didn't have an answer for that.

Konstantin turned back to Orla, and froze.

The Arab had the barrel of his Jericho 941 pressed hard against Orla's temple.

He looked a little embarrassed as he said, "The Seal, please."

THIRTY-THREE

"You." Konstantin said.

It wasn't a question.

"A man has to earn a living." The taxi driver said with a shrug.

"I'm disappointed," Konstantin said.

"But you'll get over it, I'm sure."

"Probably."

"It's been fun getting to know you, Mr Khavin."

So he knew who he was. Now it was all a just a game of sides. He wasn't with the dead men: the dead knifeman proved that. So was he an opportunist?

No.

He knew about the ring.

Konstantin knew that he hadn't mentioned it in the man's presence.

PLO?

He said nothing for a moment, but he knew the answer.

No.

He was not part of any Palestinian movement; he was far too good at doing his job for that. Job. That was the answer, of course. Konstantin hadn't once suspected the taxi driver was anything other than what he claimed to be. He should have been angry with himself. It was careless. But it also meant that there was really only one possibility.

"Mossad?" he said.

"You sound almost disappointed."

"I thought we had something," Konstantin said. "You know, special."

"You'll always be my favourite Yankee."

"So, how long have you known who I was?"

"I'm not sure if I know any more about you now than I did at the start. I was following the man who was following you. Father thought that anyone they saw as an enemy was worth keeping an eye on."

"What about the bomb?" Orla asked.

The Arab's gun didn't waver. He was quite matter of fact when he explained, "Taken care of. When I dropped your friend off, I radioed in for backup. There's a blockade at the border just waiting for them to try and take it over. Bomb disposal are waiting, too. They'll deactivate it, and have the radioactive material removed and cleanly disposed of. So the only loose end that remains is the General's ring."

"That sounds positively rude," the big Russian said.

"Please don't play games with me. Saddiq has been broadcasting a live stream out of here for the last few hours, promising he's about to rain down holy hell, raise demons and usher in Armageddon."

"Subtle," Orla said.

"He has made a spectacle of the ring, claiming it is the Seal of Solomon, which, I am sure you can appreciate, is an artefact that my people have been searching for for a very long time. It is part of our history."

"Isn't it part of theirs, too?" Orla again. She was the comparative religions expert. She understood the complexities of the Middle East far better than he did. But it sounded deliberately provocative, which, with a gun pointed at her head, might not have been the wisest course of action.

Konstantin could never quite grasp why two religions with such closely intertwined roots should have such festering animosity towards each other. Wasn't it all supposed to be love thy neighbour? The truth of course was that it seldom had anything to do with faith. It had to do with land. With power. Oppression. Difference. Faith was just a tool for manipulation. It hid the truth. He recognised the techniques. They were the Russian way. He could see Vladimir Putin, a young KGB spy at the time, disguised as a tourist in the shadow of the Kremlin's spires, with a boxy camera around his neck, while beside him, a young boy shook hands with President Reagan. The US president had just gone walkabout with Gorbachev. It was a wonderfully candid moment. Sometimes you saw your enemy in the grey steel suits, sometimes they came dressed in chinos and a polo shirt with a camera around their neck. They were still your enemy, even if you didn't recognise them.

"We cannot allow the ring to fall into the hands of our enemies," the taxi driver said. There was no shifting his position. It was more than just faith with him. "I have no wish to hurt the young lady. I think she's been through more than enough at the hands of Bashar. So, if you would be so kind as to give me the ring, I can make arrangements for the communications lockdown to be lifted, and we can all go home."

That explained a lot.

The Israelis were jamming radio signals, presumably to restrict the terrorists' communications with the outside world. No doubt, there were measures in place to keep them disconnected from the Internet, and prevent any more live streaming videos to whip up a furore among sympathisers and fury in their adversaries.

Unfortunately, one of the side effects was that it cut them off from Lethe back in Nonesuch.

"I have one question for you before I give it to you."

"Ask away."

Konstantin nodded towards Orla. Her face was swollen and bloody. "Did you do this?"

"No, my friend; I do not hit women. Unless I really have to."

"Orla?"

"He came in as I was dealing with something," she said. She didn't go into details.

"So why hold a gun to her head?"

"That's two questions, Yankee," the taxi driving Mossad agent said with a slight smile.

"Indulge me."

"Encouragement."

Konstantin nodded. "So I give you the ring and we get to walk away from here as friends?"

"Of course. Because you would have done the right thing. This is a treasure of my people. Fundamental to our faith. It is ours. It always has been. You give it to me, I take it to my bosses, and it ends up as the centrepiece in a shrine where people can come and worship it. It is the ring of our king, even if it is nothing more miraculous. So why would I want to add more bodies to this mess? No, my friend. I would much rather have this seen as a triumph for the Israeli government. I am sure you understand the politics of it. If the ring emerges in Britain, then our success becomes the success of agents of a foreign government, working without consent on our soil. This way, we have foiled a terrorist plot and rescued a precious artefact."

He was right.

It should be the Israelis' victory—but the fact that his team had been used rankled. The Israelis had abandoned their border and seemingly wanted the bomb to go off, leaving it to Orla and him to go in hot and take out Saddiq. That didn't feel good. In fact, he felt like the whore he'd left reading that trashy paperback while he slipped out the window. Used. And not in the fun way.

Konstantin slipped his hand into his pocket.

His hand closed around the ring.

"Thank you, my friend," the taxi driver said, taking it off him. "Not just from me, but from the people of Israel. You have done a good thing here tonight."

Orla's legs buckled as he let her go.

Konstantin stepped forward and caught her.

Her face was a mess. She'd lost blood, and was obviously struggling to stay focused now that her system was purging the adrenalin that had kept her going.

She said, "The spare," and was gone before he could ask her what she meant.

He carried her out of Hell.

THIRTY-FOUR

Orla woke in a hospital bed to the steady *beep* of a heart monitor.

She didn't open her eyes immediately.

She lay still, her hair matted against her scalp.

Her entire face hurt.

"Welcome back," Konstantin said. He had obviously caught the change in her breathing. She opened her eyes.

"How long?"

Konstantin glanced over at the clock. "Ten hours."

"Must have been tired."

"They tried to keep you awake. But you were having none of it. I believe the precise words were: if you don't let me sleep I'm going to get back out of this bed and kick the living crap out of you. Thank you, now good night."

She laughed, just a little, and instantly regretted it as the pain in her head amplified, finding a way through the pain killers to remind her just how much she had gone through. "Must have been the drugs talking," she said.

Orla tried to lift herself up in the bed, but quickly gave it up as a bad job.

It was better just to give into it, sometimes.

"So what now?"

"We're on the plane back to England tonight, just as long as the doc clears you to fly. The old man's sent the Gulfstream to pick us up, and he wants to see us as soon as we land."

"No rest for the wicked."

"You must have been very wicked. That's all I can say."

She raised a hand to the swelling on the side of her face, and winced as she touched it. "Born and raised in a bad town," she said. "So what's the damage?"

"Broken nose, a couple of cracked ribs, but the rest is just bruising and some tenderness. In other words, you'll live to fight another day."

She nodded. Some tenderness translated to every nerve and fibre of her being *hurt*. She knew medical speak.

"And the Seal?"

"In the possession of our friendly neighbourhood taxi driver."

"Does the old man know yet?"

"Why do you think he wants to see us?"

"Shit. Do you want to break a few more bones for me so I can play the sympathy angle?"

"It's never worked before."

"What about the bomb in the Land Rover?"

"Frosty was on hand. The Israelis stopped the Land Rover just as it crossed into Jerusalem. There were trace elements of radioactivity, but no sign of the depleted Uranium core. We missed it."

"We didn't." She said. She looked at the grazing on her knuckles. "The tyre."

"The tyre was empty."

"I switched it. There was a wreck of an old jeep abandoned near some oil drums. I swapped the spares. It's still there."

"Once we're in the air, I'll let the Israelis know. Who knows, it might even put the smile back on their faces."

"Why wouldn't they be happy? They got the win."

Konstantin tapped the side of his nose. "Let's save it until we're over international waters," the Russian said enigmatically. He wasn't saying anything else, so she let it go.

She pretended to fall asleep.

THIRTY-FIVE

It felt like forever since they'd gathered around the table.

Forever was less than a week.

Orla's pain had subsided. Now it was no more than a dull ache, and a lot of bruising to show for the beating she'd taken.

Lethe was the only one to comment on it. He made a bad joke about Max Factor. He shut up under Konstantin's withering glare.

She was there. If she'd been badly hurt, she wouldn't have been. That was all they needed to know. There was no need for cotton wool. The injuries would take time to heal, but she'd deal with that. That was the way the team functioned. Each to their own, and in their own way. It was every bit as important as the "one for all" ethos.

"Don't keep us in suspense. What happened over there?" Noah asked.

"How about you debrief us on *your* little adventure, Noah? I'm sure it was more exciting than ours."

"All in good time," Noah Larkin promised. "But first things first. Palestine?"

Konstantin said nothing.

Orla knew him well enough to know he was biding his time.

He had something to say.

He just wanted to say it when the timing was right: maximum impact.

He could be a drama queen sometimes. She smiled.

The talking stopped as the old man entered the room. He manoeuvred the chair into place at the head of the table, and acknowledged them all with a slight tilt of the head. He met Orla's stare, and offered a forced smile: one victim to another.

"The Israelis have mixed feelings about how events played out, I'm afraid. The fact that you killed everyone you came across didn't go down too well in certain quarters," he said, looking at Konstantin this time. The big Russian said nothing in his defence. Sir Charles knew that he hadn't been the only one to get his hands dirty. There was more than enough blame to share around. But he only looked at Konstantin. "They would have liked to have had the opportunity to question at least *one* of them."

"Question?" Orla said.

"Interrogate," said Frost.

"Torture," Konstantin corrected.

"One man's torture is another man's quiet little chat," Noah said.

"As I said," Sir Charles continued, "they would have preferred it if you had left at least one of them alive."

"They got the driver, didn't they?" Konstantin said.

"Ah, no," Frost said, and shrugged. It was an eloquent gesture. It spoke volumes. "He tried to make a run for it at the border. I had a choice to make."

"And the General?"

"Saves them having to deal with him," Noah said, bluntly.

"He's the head of the snake. There will always be another one like him growing. They are concerned we have turned him into a spiritual martyr."

"Bollocks," the Russian said, sounding very, very English. "He was a madman."

"Little difference, sometimes," the old man said.

"And if he was in one of their jails instead of six feet under, there'd be a spate of kidnappings until they found a bargaining piece valuable enough to secure his release. It's not like it hasn't happened before. Sometimes, dead's best."

"Indeed, Mr Frost," Sir Charles said. "Control suspects that the Israelis intend to arrange a controlled explosion to make it appear that Saddiq's men not only failed in their attempt to detonate a dirty bomb at the Wailing Wall, but died of their own incompetence in the process. No one will mourn them then, at least not on the Jerusalem side of the divide."

"The Uranium?" Orla began. She had no problem with the idea of a controlled explosion, especially if it destroyed the compound.

"Safely contained. Konstantin's taxi driving friend delivered the message." It wasn't quite a dressing down, but given the fact that an undercover Mossad agent had driven the Russian around the city for a couple of days, it was worth a grin—even if Lethe was the only one who struggled to keep the smile from his lips.

"What I don't get is, how come the Israelis aren't crowing about the fact that they've recovered their long-lost treasure?" Noah said. "It's not like them to keep quiet about anything, especially when it gives them the chance to rub the Muslims' collective noses in it."

Orla knew something was not quite right about the whole thing, but she hadn't pushed Konstantin, even when they were up in the air.

"Unless they haven't got it," Frost said.

Orla shook her head. "I saw Konstantin hand it over. He took it from Saddiq and—"

"It was a fake," the Russian said. "Sleight of hand. He expected a ring; I gave him a ring. I didn't give him *the* ring."

There was silence.

Lots of it.

The old man held out a hand to Konstantin.

Konstantin said nothing.

He reached into his pocket and pulled the Seal of Solomon out. He placed the battered gold ring in Sir Charles' outstretched hand. It was not the most impressive of relics: a small circle of gold, bent out of shape by centuries lying underground. The Star of David was only faintly visible, but it was there.

"Is it real?" Noah asked.

"I believe so," the old man said.

"I don't understand," Orla said.

"We had two objectives," the Russian said. "Prevent the dirty bomb from being driven into Israel, and keep the ring out of the hands of the Israelis. Why give them something else to kill each other over?"

"In a few days, they will release the results of tests that reveal that the ring was a medieval fake." Sir Charles explained with a twinkle in his eye. "Old, yes; but still a fake." Sir Charles explained with a twinkle in his eye.

Orla looked at the Russian, "Where the hell did you manage to find a fake when we were over there? You could hardly pop out to the local jewellers and ask for one."

"There are benefits to being a collector of rare antiquities, my dear," the old man replied for him. "One of them is an empty tray downstairs marked Seal of Solomon, Medieval Replica, circa AD 800."

"And we want the whole world to think that the real thing hasn't been found," Orla suggested. "Because no matter which museum it goes into, it's going to become a target for every faction, every extremist group, every zealot and nut-job out there."

The old man nodded. "You are quite right. It would make the arguments over the Stone of Destiny, the Elgin Marbles, Hell's Teeth, even the Dome of the Rock, seem like petty squabbles."

"Quite handy that there's an empty tray downstairs marked Seal of Solomon, Medieval Replica, circa AD 800, then," Lethe said.

"That it is, Mr Lethe. That it is."

THE END

THE OGMIOS DIRECTIVE

Crucible

Steven Savile & Steve Lockley

Solomon's Seal

Steven Savile & Steve Lockley

Lucifer's Machine

Steven Savile & Rick Chesler

Wargod

Steven Savile & Sean Ellis

Shining Ones

Steven Savile & Richard Salter

Argo

Steven Savile & Ashley Knight

Lightning Source UK Ltd.
Milton Keynes UK
UKOW05f1816190317
296919UK00007B/29/P